The EINSTEINS of VISTA POINT

Also by
BEN GUTERSON

THE WINTERHOUSE TRILOGY

Winterhouse
The Secrets of Winterhouse
The Winterhouse Mysteries

The
EINSTEINS
of VISTA
POINT

BEN GUTERSON

Illustrated by PETUR ANTONSSON

Christy Ottaviano Books

LITTLE, BROWN AND COMPANY

New York Boston

Text copyright © 2022 by Ben Guterson
Illustrations copyright © 2022 by Petur Antonsson

Cover art copyright © 2022 by Vivienne To. Cover design by Sasha Illingworth.
Cover copyright © 2022 by Hachette Book Group, Inc.

Christy Ottaviano Books
Hachette Book Group
1290 Avenue of the Americas, New York, NY 10104
Visit us at LBYR.com

First Edition: April 2022

Christy Ottaviano Books is an imprint of Little, Brown and Company. The Christy Ottaviano Books name and logo are trademarks of Hachette Book Group, Inc.

The publisher is not responsible for websites (or their content) that are not owned by the publisher.

Library of Congress Cataloging-in-Publication Data
Names: Guterson, Ben, author. | Antonsson, Petur.
Title: The Einsteins of Vista Point / Ben Guterson ; illustrated by Petur Antonsson.
Description: First edition. | New York ; Boston : Little, Brown and Company, 2022. |
"Christy Ottaviano Books." | Audience: Ages 8–12. | Summary: Eager for a fresh start,
the grieving Einstein family moves to the remote town of Vista Point to
renovate an old house and turn it into a bed-and-breakfast.
Identifiers: LCCN 2021012487 | ISBN 9780316317436 (hardcover) |
ISBN 9780316317634 (ebook)
Subjects: CYAC: Brothers and sisters—Fiction. | Grief—Fiction. | Family life—Fiction. |
Spirits—Fiction. | Jews—Fiction.
Classification: LCC PZ7.1.G885 Ei 2022 | DDC [Fic]—dc23
LC record available at https://lccn.loc.gov/2021012487

ISBNs: 978-0-316-31743-6 (hardcover), 978-0-316-31763-4 (ebook)

Printed in the United States of America

LSC-C

Printing 1, 2022

For

MARGARET MICKELSON, SALLY ALGER,
MARGARET IMPETT, AND ANNABEL BLACK,
DEVOTED TEACHERS FROM MY BOYHOOD DAYS

I once wrote down this sentence in a journal, but I can't for the life of me recall where I read it: "I know more than I can express in words, and the little I can express would not have been expressed, had I not known more." That line always makes me think of a dear friend I lost.

From *The Wonderful World of Words!* by Dylan Grimes

CONTENTS

One

THE GIRL FROM THE WOODS

Zack Einstein was reading his favorite novel, *Falcons and Bandits*, when he looked out the open window of his room and saw a girl walking toward the abandoned Tower. He shot up from his bed, fumbling the book to the floor with a smack that echoed through the house.

"You okay?" Zack's father yelled from the kitchen below.

"Just dropped my book, Dad," Zack called, keeping his eyes fixed on the girl heading for the stone building in the distance. It seemed she had emerged from the thick cover of hemlocks west of the Tower, something that was very odd, given that the building was strictly off-limits to everyone and was just on the other side of the property the Einstein family now owned. But what astonished

Zack most of all was that the ponytailed girl looked—from far away, at least—like Susan, his sister who was gone forever.

Zack stared. The girl's hair was red, her jeans were light blue, and her white shirt hung loosely from her tiny shoulders—all in uncanny imitation of Zack's little sister.

Why is she going to the Tower? he thought.

And then, although he'd tried to stave it off, came the question he'd asked himself countless times over the past ten months: *Why didn't I watch out for Susan?*

For half an hour he'd been able to lose himself in a book he loved, and now thoughts of his sister had returned to him like rain resuming.

"As long as the book's okay," his father yelled. When Zack said nothing in return, his father added: "That's a joke, son."

"Okay, Dad," Zack called just as the girl stepped behind the stone building and disappeared from view. He stared, waited.

The Tower, a hundred yards to the north and taller than the third-story window through which Zack was watching, stood in all its solitary majesty near the edge of the bluff. On the far side of the Tower, an immense hill sloped to the river below. It was an impressive building, nine-sided and rimmed with graceful, sturdy columns; though after Ruth—the closest in age to Zack, two years older than his eleven—had said it looked like a gigantic cake with gray frosting, the image had been hard for him to get out of his mind. There was no official name for the building, as far as any of the kids knew. Miriam, herself two years older than Ruth, had suggested they call it "the big thimble" when their parents brought them to Vista Point three months before for their first visit. ("We'll be living here come summer," their mother had explained.) Once Ethan, the oldest of the siblings at sixteen, had dubbed it "the Tower," the name had stuck.

When the girl did not reappear after a long minute, Zack imagined she was standing before the front doors of the Tower and taking in the impressive view on the opposite side: the quarter-mile-wide

Grand River, the range of mountains to the northeast, the thick forest on both sides and across the water, the clear sky above. From that spot, everything was deep blue or lush emerald, endless and broad. The girl was most likely admiring all of it, just as Zack and his brother and sisters had done every day since they'd moved to Vista Point five days before. Their new house was only an hour away from Roseburg, the only place they'd ever called home, but it might as well have been in another country. Vista Point was a speck on the map, more a community of scattered houses and large plots of land, while Roseburg was the biggest city in the state.

"A fresh start will do us all good," Zack's mother and father had said so many times over the past several weeks that Zack had begun to wonder if they believed it or if they mainly wanted him and his siblings to believe it.

During the previous winter, his parents had found a fixer-upper put up for sale by an elderly couple who could no longer maintain the home or the property, and now the future was starkly laid out: The Einsteins would be turning the bottom floor of their new house into a bed-and-breakfast, something Zack had come to understand was sort of like a small hotel set up in a regular home. Why his father had quit his architect's job at the Valencia & Hartnett Firm to serve people scrambled eggs and change their bedsheets—and why Zack's mother seemed just as eager to join in, abandoning her teacher-training coursework at Roseburg Community College—was something that didn't seem to add up. He couldn't understand their enthusiasm for the move or why they'd become intent on relocating to the middle of nowhere.

"I think Mom and Dad feel we won't be so sad about Susan if we move," Miriam had once told him, but Zack couldn't get the words to make sense.

Zack continued to stare out his window, yet the girl did not reappear. He wondered if maybe she had descended the slope and then circled back into the forest, which would be the surest way of departing—or approaching—the Tower if a person didn't want to be seen from the house. Zack glanced at his clock: 3:17. His mother and his siblings had gone to the nearby small town of Thornton Falls for the afternoon and weren't due to return for another hour. They'd all pressed Zack to join them—his father, too, had encouraged him to get out—but, as had been his habit ever since the awful night the previous August, he was more comfortable staying in his room and reading. He had no desire to be around people, around crowds.

"First day of summer's a good time to explore, Z," Ethan—only three merit badges from becoming an Eagle Scout—had told him at lunch by way of encouraging him to join them on their afternoon outing. "You should come with us. There's a map store we could check out."

"I'm taking the basketball, Zack," Miriam, the athlete of the bunch, had said when Zack had indicated he was going to stay home. "We could play H-O-R-S-E. I'll even show you my new crossover move."

"Or we could all compose poems under the gazebo in the town square," Ruth had said, giving her sister a well-practiced and exaggeratedly eager look, because she knew writing was the last thing Miriam would want to do—and Miriam had goggled her eyes right back, all in good fun.

Zack understood and even appreciated that his siblings went out of their way to try to include him—and make him laugh. He just wasn't in the mood to be cheered up. Ever.

Now all he could think about was that he had another hour to himself, and the girl who looked like Susan was out there somewhere near the Tower. He waited a minute, and then another minute, watching all the while. The thought came to him that maybe the girl was lost—or maybe she had tried to go inside or had even hurt herself somehow. That she had gone to the Tower and was still out of sight was worrying him. Zack glanced at his clock once more, looked back at the Tower, and then slipped on his shoes and departed his room, hopping quickly down the stairs.

"Gonna go outside for a few, Dad," he called as he dashed for the front door.

"Don't be gone long," his father said. But Zack was already out the door and heading for the Tower, thinking as he began to jog: *Maybe that girl needs help.*

— *Two* —

THE FORBIDDEN TOWER

The Tower was absolutely forbidden to the four Einstein kids. They were allowed to admire it from the outside—the clean lines of gray sandstone bricks that made up its walls, the precise planes of its nine sides, the gentle arches of the now mostly boarded-up windows—and even sit on the stone stairs in front of its enormous metal doors; but, as their parents had made clear to them, the Tower wasn't part of what they owned, and they were to make no attempt to go inside. Not that doing so would be possible—the doors were locked tight (though none of the four kids had dared test this), and several No Trespassing signs were posted on the building. The place certainly looked abandoned— its windows were covered, and the masonry of its outer walls was chipped and flaking in spots and mildewed in broad patches— though all the Einstein kids had agreed it didn't appear quite as run-down as their parents had led them to believe before they'd seen it for themselves.

"This must have been the coolest rest stop ever," Ruth had said when the four of them visited the Tower on the day of their arrival. "So scenic, so romantic. The kind of place I could write about." She looked around wistfully and then said, "*When Bridgette Carlisle gazed out at the river from the Vista Point Tower, she knew she would love Thomas Cooper forever.*"

"No one would read that story," Ethan had said, shaking his head and turning to point—his arm fixed straight and steady—upriver. "Interesting. From here, Mount Knox is almost exactly at a forty-five-degree angle." He took his compass out of his pocket and began to fiddle with it.

Miriam pantomimed a jump shot in the air. "Forty-five degrees when the ball leaves my hands," she said, and Ruth sighed heavily. Miriam called out, "And that's a three-pointer for the win!" as she stared at an imaginary hoop, and then she stopped and peered downward to the river far below and the strip of highway that ran just beside it.

"I wish they hadn't built the highway down there," she said. "Dad says if they hadn't, the old road up here would still be the only one through, and people would still be traveling by and stopping here. The Tower never would have gotten so run-down."

Zack, however, wasn't thinking back to that visit from a few days before just now—he had slowed his run and was striding closer to the stone building, keeping his eyes out for any sign of movement. He was keenly aware that his father might be watching him from the kitchen window, far behind him on the other side of the big field that separated their house from the Tower. He veered off to the west, close to the forest that bordered the field, and drew near the bluff; and then he trotted down the slope a short way, deliberately overshooting the Tower and glancing at its front stairs as he did. No one was in sight. Zack came to a stop and turned around. The slope now blocked his view of the house—and ensured that his father could not see him—as Zack studied the building. All was silent beneath the high, hot sun, and Zack felt not only all alone but very distant suddenly, as though his new house were miles away.

The memory came to him once again from late August of the year before.

All seven of the Einsteins had gone to the Western State Fair, south of Roseburg, near the town of Hugard. Zack and Susan, his younger sister by two years, had stayed with their mother while the others had scattered to enjoy the rides and sights and booths; Ethan and their father had stayed together, and the two older girls had gone off on their own. By eight o'clock, with twilight deepening and the strains of a country music band wafting from the arena at the center of the fairgrounds, Zack and Susan were sharing cotton candy while their mother led them to the gate and out to the street that lined the way. The three of them stopped and waited beside the chain-link fence, noise and lights and people and cars moving in a swirl of motion before them. A huge WELCOME TO THE 2001 WESTERN STATE FAIR! banner was strung between two high poles just before them.

"Where are they?" Zack's mother said after a short while, scanning for the others. "They should be here."

Susan plucked at a wisp of cotton candy clumped on the stiff paper stick Zack held, and the two of them giggled and smacked away happily. Zack felt his mouth and cheeks becoming sticky from the pink sugar. His mother appeared worried as she glanced about.

"Wait right here, you two," she said, giving Zack a severe look. She pointed to the gate just off to their right. "Maybe they thought we were meeting inside." And with another hard stare at Zack, she said, "Don't move from this fence, okay? I'll be right back."

Susan was focused on the cotton candy; but then she stopped plucking at the sugary wisps, gave Zack a sly look, and said, "Susan sees a man wearing purple flip-flops." She lifted her chin to look skyward, her typical way of confounding Zack whenever they played this game.

"Right there!" Zack said almost immediately, pointing to a man who'd just passed them and who was, indeed, wearing purple flip-flops. They both loved this game, all the more so because it always seemed to exasperate their siblings.

"And now Zack sees a woman holding two caramel apples and a hot dog," he said.

"I see her!" Susan said. "Gosh, remember last year when you ate two hot dogs before we rode the roller coaster?"

Zack clutched his stomach theatrically. "Don't remind me!"

As Susan reached to snatch another shred off the stick Zack held, a kitten appeared from behind a plywood program stand beside them.

"Look!" Susan said, pointing to the tiny gray cat. She knelt to reach out to it as Zack watched; and then she jerked her hand too quickly, and the small thing darted off.

"Oh no!" Susan called as the kitten skipped through the mass of people passing on the sidewalk—and before Zack could stop her, Susan was racing away.

"Hey!" he yelled, but she was gone, following the tiny cat; the last image he had was of his sister—in her blue shorts and her favorite white sweater—frantically chasing a kitten. After that, his memories were only of a weirdly dark sky, the squealing of car tires, an awful thud, and then what sounded like a thousand people shouting all around him.

The moments from that point on were pure chaos, and he never could recall how his mother—and then his father and his siblings—had found him or how he understood Susan was missing, and everyone seemed to be crying or in shock or feeling some other emotion he couldn't understand. In fact, as hard as he tried to remember the details of what had happened after Susan rushed away, his mind couldn't make any sense of it. How he'd ended up back at his house and what happened later that night—none of it remained with him. There were days of strange sadness, and then a funeral, and then weeks of nothing more than sitting in his room or lying on his bed; he still couldn't remember what had happened or what he'd done during that time, though eventually he returned to school and the days continued marching forward. He only knew that Susan would never be coming back—and he felt absolutely that the reason for this was that he'd let her follow the kitten. There had been something he had failed to do or some part of him that had caused things to unfold as they had.

"I never should have left the two of you alone," Zack's mother would often say whenever she took him up in a tearful embrace. "Never." But he always felt she was only trying to make him feel less sad by claiming it was her fault. He knew better. He'd not watched his little sister as carefully as he should have. His mother or his father or Ethan or the girls could say whatever they liked— he knew the truth of things.

Zack gazed at the Grand River below. A bridge, the only one within twenty miles up or down the broad river, spanned the water to the east, though it was so far away and so far beneath him, the cars on it moved soundlessly, like small toys on a distant track. For that matter, the water itself appeared to move slowly enough from up here that the river looked like a long, motionless strip of blue that stretched to each horizon. Unbroken forest covered the hills on the opposite shore, so distant that the trees merged into a single cover of thick green. Zack studied the Tower once again. *The girl must have gone back into the woods*, he thought.

The gray building looked imposing in the sunlight, both graceful and sturdy, and Zack considered how perfect it must have been before the tall windows were boarded up and the tiles on its roof cap had become frayed or torn loose. It was hard to believe, now that he'd visited the Tower a few times, that it had been allowed to fall into disrepair like this. He squinted and tried to picture the building as it had once been.

Something moved inside.

At a window—just barely visible through the wooden boards covering it—on the upper level of the Tower, a silhouette appeared momentarily, a shadow that passed so quickly, Zack couldn't be sure his eyes hadn't played a trick on him. He waited and watched, but nothing more appeared; he took several steps toward the Tower, scanning the upper windows all the while. And as he drew closer to the stairs, he saw something he could hardly believe: The doors to the stone building were slightly ajar.

Zack walked softly up the few steps. In the space created where the doors had been left open, he saw a thin portion of the inside of the Tower, shadowy and dim, with only a bit of light from the few windows high above. He put his hand on one of the doors and turned his head to listen within. No sound came. Zack leaned closer to the crack in the doorway and saw muted light gleaming off a marble floor. He glanced at the river one more time, and then he gave a slow pull on one of the doors and entered the Tower.

— *Three* —

A NEW FRIEND

It took a moment for Zack's eyes to adjust to the dimness inside, but once they did, he was dazzled by what he saw. Aside from the white marble floor—so pure and delicate, Zack almost felt he was hovering on air—the walls were smooth and held a light-pink hue. He'd assumed they would be gray sandstone, simply the other face of the bricks on the outside; but these walls were seamless and clean, as though they'd been painted just the week before. The stone ribs of the insides of the columns rose up and around Zack on all sides; and although the window openings on the first level were covered in plywood, a few unbroken windows—done in panes of green and yellow glass—high up on the second level allowed in a delicate light that gave the entire interior a spectral glow. It was like being in a deep part of the forest late in the day with tall cedars all around, when the air is a pleasant and soft emerald and everything feels quiet and still. What was most remarkable, though, was that the inside of the Tower wasn't a fraction as grubby or run-down as Zack would have guessed, particularly given the condition of the exterior—in fact, the inside looked almost perfect, as though it had been closed up one day and had suffered hardly at all in the time since.

Zack stared upward at the golden-tiled domed ceiling. At its very center—the highest and farthest point from where Zack stood—was something round and silvery that looked a bit like a very flat smoke detector, though this seemed so out of place that Zack was certain he was mistaken. He looked more closely, and an unaccountable feeling of intrigue came over him. The thing—whatever it was—glinted in the faint light as Zack shifted his head to get a better view. It was, it seemed, some sort of large medallion set in the very midpoint of the ceiling, though the light was too faint to let him make out any detail. Zack was curious, powerfully so, about what it was.

He scanned downward from the dome's peak. Between the two levels of the Tower's interior, set in a circle around the rim dividing the sections, were small sculptures—plaques, Zack realized, faces of what appeared to be people from long ago: Native Americans in headdress, pioneers, settlers, soldiers in peaked caps. As Zack turned to look at each one, he noticed a narrow marble staircase against the wall to his left, and his eyes traveled up to where it reached the second level. There, just above the railing, the girl with the ponytail of red hair was staring down at him.

"Hi," she said softly, greeting him with a hesitant, barely raised hand. The shadows were so deep where she stood, it was difficult for him to see her.

"Hi," Zack answered as he lifted a hand in return. There was something so easy and natural about the girl's voice and the way she acknowledged him that Zack wasn't startled or surprised at all. As he gazed upward, Zack thought the girl would say something, but she only clutched the railing before her and kept looking down at him.

"How did you get in here?" Zack said. His voice echoed in the airy space.

The girl pointed to the door Zack had left open behind him. "I just came in," she said with a soft shrug.

"It wasn't locked?" Even as he spoke the words, Zack mentally reviewed the handful of times he and his siblings had visited the Tower, and realized they'd never once tried the doors. They might not have been locked at all.

The girl shook her head. "No. I just came in. I've been outside lots of times before, but this is the first time I've been inside."

"We just moved here," Zack blurted out. "I mean, me and my family."

"You live in the big house over there?" she said, pointing.

"Yeah. My name's Zack. We used to live in Roseburg."

"I'm Ann."

Zack glanced at the doors once again. "Are you by yourself?"

She nodded, and then, with a tug on the railing to stretch her chin over its top, she said, "You should come up here and take a look."

Zack moved quickly to the stairs and skipped up them, and then he was standing just before Ann and marveling, once again, at how much she resembled Susan—her red hair, her ponytail, her big brown eyes. She was even about Susan's height.

"I *thought* I saw someone in here when I was outside," Zack said. "And it was you."

Ann smiled with her lips pressed tightly together, and she nodded with excitement. "I thought I saw someone outside. And it was you!" She gave a little shrug and looked as delighted as if Zack had brought candy for them to share. "At first I thought you were a boy I know from school, because you have bushy black hair like him. And you're skinny, too."

Zack felt himself smiling at Ann in return. "How old are you?" he said.

"Nine."

"I'm eleven," he said.

"One and one. Wow!"

Zack laughed. "My birthday was in October. When's yours?"

"May fifth."

"Cinco de Mayo."

"What?" Ann said.

"It's a holiday."

"It's my birthday."

Zack laughed once more, but only because Ann spoke so bluntly, so sincerely. "You live near here?" he said.

Ann nodded. "Vista Point is the best. There's waterfalls and places to swim and trails. I love to hike around and explore. That's one of my favorite things to do." She glanced over the side of the railing. "I like it in here. I always wanted to see inside."

"I just didn't know we could get in," Zack said. "I thought it would be falling apart, but it's pretty nice here."

"It really is." She began examining the ceiling, her mouth dropping open. "Quiet, too."

"How far away do you live?" Zack said.

"Just on the other side of the woods."

"Your parents let you go out alone?"

"I know every trail around here," Ann said, which, Zack thought, didn't really answer his question. "*And* all the good places to swim. I've always lived in Vista Point."

Neither spoke for a moment, and a deep hush held inside the Tower. Zack glanced at the medallion in the ceiling; there appeared to be words written on it.

"Do you have any brothers or sisters?" Ann said. "I don't."

"One brother and three sisters," Zack said. He paused. "But the youngest sister isn't here with us anymore." And then, because he felt he'd revealed something—partway, at least—that he didn't

19

want to explain, he said, "The others are with my mom, shopping in Thornton Falls."

Ann was looking at him; she seemed to be waiting for him to go on speaking. "What do you mean, she's not with you anymore?" she said.

"She had a bad accident last summer," Zack said. He glanced at the ceiling.

"Oh, I'm sorry," Ann said, and the Tower became silent once more. Ann stretched her neck over the railing and swept her eyes slowly over the walls and marble floor of the Tower, a deliberate and steady survey.

"You okay?" Zack said, turning to her.

She looked at him and gave a tiny, reassuring smile. Her teeth were slightly crooked, which made her look a bit younger than nine, Zack thought.

"What's your favorite thing to eat?" she said. "Mine is oatmeal with chocolate chips in it. It's so good!"

Zack laughed loudly—Ann's question had been completely unexpected.

"My favorite thing to eat?" he said. "I guess German chocolate cake. My mom always makes it for me on my birthday, and my dad says it's lucky to eat that kind of cake, but I think he's just making that up."

"My mother told me this place is lucky," she said.

"Lucky? This building?"

"Yes, lucky for all the people around here." Ann swept an arm before her to indicate, it seemed, not just the Tower but outside as well. "Everything."

"It's cool to live near it," Zack said. He didn't quite understand what Ann had tried to explain. "It's just right on the other side of our property."

"Then you could come here anytime!"

A pang of guilt ran through Zack. "My parents don't want me to come inside. Me or my brother or sisters. They would be mad if they found out."

"Well, maybe you could talk to them. Get their permission? What was your name again?"

"Zack."

"Zack," she said, as if testing out the sound of his name. "I thought you said Jack at first."

"No, Zack."

"It rhymes with lots of things. *Back, sack, rack.* I like to make poems. At school and at home." With a quick jab of her hand, she pointed upward at the medallion. "Hey, I was looking at something up there before you came. Did you see that?"

"I saw it when I came in."

"I thought I saw you looking at it!" Ann said. She reached for his hand and began walking around the rim of the second level until, just a few steps ahead, they came to a spot where the light from a window shone more directly on the medallion.

"You can see it better from here," Ann said. "Can you read what it says? My vision isn't so great."

Zack peered at the medallion, a flat disk—maybe eight or nine inches across—of what appeared to be silver or nickel on which were three rings of "words" (though they didn't look like any words Zack had ever seen) circling three actual words at the center. It looked like this:

"It doesn't make any sense," Zack said. "It's just, like, random letters."

Ann was still gazing up at the ceiling. "I don't know," she said. "But it's…"

She went silent, though Zack thought he understood what she was getting at. It wasn't just that the words and the medallion seemed peculiar—as he'd read the lines to himself, he'd felt unexpectedly at ease, if only momentarily, in a way he couldn't recall feeling for a while.

"It's *interesting*," Zack said, a word his father used often to describe things he couldn't quite explain.

"That's it," Ann said. "It's interesting."

A call arose from far off: "Zack!"

"That's my dad!" Zack said. He realized he'd been away for at least twenty minutes now.

"Zack!" came his father's voice again.

The two kids clomped down the stairs and made for the doors without a word. When they were in the sunlight once more, Zack pushed the doors closed and yelled, "Coming, Dad!"

He turned to Ann. "I'm at home most of the time, so you can come over if you want. But I can't let my dad see us coming out of here." He gestured downward to indicate they'd need to descend and then circle back up to the top of the bluff, but some distance from the Tower.

"I don't want you to get in trouble," Ann said, and then she widened her eyes as a thought came to her. "And I don't want to get in trouble, either!"

"I won't say anything," Zack said. "I won't even tell them I met you, okay?"

"Zack!" his father called. "Where are you?"

Ann nodded. "Okay. But let's meet here again."

Zack held out a hand to her. "That's a deal."

She broke into a huge smile and shot her hand at him to shake. "Deal!"

"Coming!" Zack yelled.

He and Ann moved slightly downhill and then swerved to the right. After several paces, Zack turned uphill and Ann continued on toward the trees without looking back.

"Zack!" his dad yelled, even more insistently this time. "Where are you?"

Zack darted up the hill a few steps and lifted a hand to wave. His father was in front of the house in the distance.

"Right here!" Zack called. "I'm fine. Coming!"

He looked downhill and watched Ann disappear into the forest. She looked so much like Susan in that moment, trotting away from him, that Zack felt his breath catch. Just as remarkable, though, was that he realized he'd actually laughed two or three times with her. It seemed like a long time since he'd felt that light, that easy.

He stared at the dense row of cedars and hemlocks before him.

I hope I see her again tomorrow, he thought.

— Four —

DINNER DISCUSSIONS

The Einsteins had never been the sort of family to celebrate the Sabbath—or, as they generally called it, Shabbat—on Friday evenings. But the previous October, right around the time Zack resumed school after missing the first month, his mother and father began marking the start of each Friday's dinner by lighting two candles and saying a prayer or two, and then everyone spoke a few words about Susan. Zack, for reasons he couldn't quite make clear to himself, had never contributed any thoughts about his sister during those moments. Tonight, the first Friday dinner in their new home, would be extra special, Zack understood, and he'd been looking forward to it.

The house needed a lot of work, no doubt, but even Zack—who'd been the least enthusiastic of all about moving—had to confess that the place was impressive: "a three-story Victorian-style mansion," as his father liked to say, with ten bedrooms, ceilings that were twice as high as the ones in their house in Roseburg, a porch that wrapped around most of the house, and seven gables on the roof—"for seven Einsteins," Ethan noted. There was siding to fix and a roof to patch and gutters to replace and so much painting and cleaning to do inside that the work seemed as though it would be endless; but now that they had officially moved in, all the Einsteins, to one degree or another, marveled at how spacious and lovely the house was.

"Morton, you light the candles tonight," Zack's mother said to his father, who scratched his bushy black beard and looked perplexed.

"But I did it last week," he said. "It's your turn. We always take turns." He snatched up the little matchbook that lay on the white tablecloth and pretended to read the back of it: "On this, the first day of summer, Deborah Einstein, expert chef and someday a great elementary school teacher, shall recite the Shabbat prayer in the presence of her family. About this she must not dispute with her loving husband."

"It doesn't say that!" she said, plucking the matchbook from her husband's hands as the two of them began to laugh.

Zack's father was tall and lanky, with a full head of hair and a beard he'd allowed to grow a little too long, Zack thought, over the past few months. His mother, on the other hand, was so short that Zack was taller than she was, and he wasn't exactly out of the ordinary for someone about to start seventh grade in the fall. She had reddish hair (Susan had been the only one of the kids to take after their mother in that regard) and delicate hands and eyes that sloped in a way that tended to make her look a little sad, something that had deepened recently.

"I'll do it!" Miriam said with mock exasperation, and she took the matchbook from her mother and positioned herself before the two white candles.

"Crisis averted," Zack's father said, and Miriam flashed a proud grin as she pretended to shake her nonexistent mane of hair with regal pomp. This was a frequent joke with her, given that she had the shortest hair in the family, a tight little bob she insisted was necessary so that it didn't get in the way when she played basketball.

"You know, after you light a match," Ethan said, "you need to make sure it's completely out before you set it down. As my scout-master always used to say, most forest fires start because people are careless with matches." He paused. "Just saying."

Miriam gazed around the room as if she'd spotted a bee buzzing about. "Is this a forest?" she said dryly.

"*Miriam Einstein didn't mean to set the house on fire that tragic Friday evening*," Ruth began. "It could be a great story!"

"Enough!" their father said. "It's prayer time." He looked at Miriam as he reached to flick off the light switch. "Let's get it going."

Miriam struck a match aflame, gave a spooky little look at Ethan to emphasize that no inferno had begun, and then touched the match to the wicks of the two white candles before shaking it out dramatically. She waved her hands grandly over the candles, something she'd seen her grandmother on their father's side do many times, as if to fan the flames or heighten the mood.

"Blessed are you," she said, "Lord our God, King—or *Queen*—of the universe…"

"Why can't you just say *ruler* if you want it to be even?" Ruth whispered.

"Let her finish," their mother said.

"*Ruler* of the universe," Miriam said. "Who creates the lights of the fire." She looked up triumphantly. "Amen!"

"Amen!" everyone echoed as their mother and father kissed each other, and then they all grew quiet and kept their eyes on the flickering candle flames. The chandelier overhead, a frilly spray of rusted bronze and dewdrop lights, was unilluminated, and the darkly paneled dining room was dim in the candlelight.

"I can't believe in a couple of months it will be a full year," Ruth said. "I miss her."

"Sometimes I think I can almost hear her voice again," Ethan said. "Her little lisp."

"I don't know how I'm going to feel when August gets here," their mother said. She looked to her husband. "I'm grateful we have this project ahead of us with the house. This new life. Susan would have loved it here. She would have…" But before their mother could continue her sentence, she clamped both hands to her eyes and began to weep.

Their father enfolded her in his arms, and no one said a word. Zack stared at his plate and felt the tears welling in his eyes, too.

His mother's gentle sobbing continued as his father whispered to her, something soft and reassuring.

After a moment, his mother lowered her hands and sighed with finality. "I'm okay," she said dully. "I'm fine. I'm sorry for that. It's just..."

"We know, Mom," Ethan said gently. "It's okay. We all understand."

The silence resumed. No one looked away from the candles.

"Zack?" his father said. "Want to say anything?"

A moment passed. Zack sat, not moving or looking up. His mother came to him and hugged his neck from behind without speaking, and then she pulled away and turned on the lights. In as chipper a voice as she could muster, she said, "Green curry with chicken for the nonvegetarians. I'm talking to everyone besides Ruth. It's my newest recipe, so go easy on me." And with that, she and Ethan began bringing the food to the table, Ruth moved the candles to the bureau off to one side, and everyone settled in for their fifth dinner in their new house.

Between the time Zack had returned from the Tower and dinner—even as Ethan regaled him with stories about the map store and a nearby skate park—Zack had been unable to take his mind off his meeting with Ann. Beyond the unexpected magnificence of the inside of the Tower and the mystery of the strange medallion affixed to its ceiling, Ann had cheered him up. For the first time in months,

Zack felt a little less unhappy. Whereas all the past summers of his life had been full of promise and excitement, this one had felt as though it would be a continuation of the gray days he'd lived through for months—until the afternoon that had just passed.

"Dad," Zack said, during a lull in the conversation, "why did people stop visiting the Tower?"

Zack's father looked to their mother, who put her fork down and said, "It was built over a hundred years ago, you know, so it's pretty old. From what we've found out, the general upkeep on it was kind of spotty for a long time because of money problems. It was going to be a great observation point, but then it became mostly a rest stop, unfortunately."

"Now freeways just have tiny pull-offs and a Sani-Kan," Miriam said. "If you're lucky."

"That's not quite true, Babe Didrikson," their father said.

Miriam sighed with exaggeration. "Dad, at least call me someone still alive. That woman was an athlete, like, in the eighteenth century."

Ethan laughed and said, "You, history buff—how Miriam gets all her dates mixed up."

This way of phrasing things had become a running family joke ever since their parents had decided to move to Vista Point. They'd purchased a book entitled *You, Innkeeper—How to Organize and Manage Your Very Own Bed-and-Breakfast Establishment*; and although it had proven to be a great guide for understanding the work that lay ahead, its title had become the template for countless wisecracks. "You, bagel eater," their father would say when he came upon one of the kids eating lunch. "How to spread cream cheese on your sesame seed bagel." Or "You, socks-on-the-floor-leaver," their mother would say to Ruth when she surveyed her messy room. "How to drive your parents crazy and make your room stink in one easy step."

"Anyway," their father said, continuing the conversation about the Tower, "the only road through here used to be right on our property. It was the highway. Very little trace of it now. But then they built the main road down there along the river about thirty years ago, and there was some dispute about access to the Tower up here, and I guess it just sort of shut down and became neglected. It never turned into as big a deal as they thought it would. It's a shame."

"There's a historical society that goes in and cleans it occasionally," their mother said, "so it doesn't rot away. They own it. I'd love to have them open it for us one of these days so we can take a peek."

"It looks so cool from the outside," Ethan said.

You should see the inside, Zack wanted to say.

"Just be careful when you go there," their father said. "First, it's not on our property, though it's not really trespassing just to admire it. Still, I wouldn't want a wall to topple over on you."

"You've seen it, Dad," Miriam said. "It's not in bad shape."

"We should fix it up," Zack said. Everyone stopped eating and looked to him, and Zack realized he'd spoken with a degree of enthusiasm he rarely displayed, at least recently. He glanced around. "I mean, we don't own it, but maybe we could? And make it nice again?"

Their mother gestured to the ceiling as if to direct Zack's attention to it. "The house is going to take up all our energy for now."

"And money," their father said through a humorous little cough as he glanced at his plate.

"And money." Their mother smiled at Zack. "But I think it's a good idea, trying to do something about the Tower someday. Who knows? If we ever got ambitious and the historical society wanted it off their hands?" She made a check mark in the air. "Future project!"

She'd meant well, but something about the way she phrased things—as an effort to be considered at some far-off point—deflated him, and he returned to eating his meal in silence.

"Seriously," Miriam said, looking to her parents, "do you really think we'll have this house in shape by Labor Day? That's less than three months from now." She turned left and then right and then glanced upward before settling her gaze again. "We have a long way to go."

Their father tapped his head. "That's the genius of Morton Einstein right there. We'll be opening up right when things are slowing down. That way we can ease into the business."

His wife gave him a deadpan smile. "Sort of a joint brainstorm there," she said before turning to the kids. "But, yeah, that's the plan. One of the things we learned from the book."

"Something else we wanted to mention," their father said. "We've heard there's a kind of camp out in the woods where people are living."

"It's a commune," their mother said. "You know, a group of

people living kind of independently. Living off the land, I think."

"Hippies?" Ruth said excitedly. "Hippies live in the woods near our house? That's so cool. I always wanted to meet hippies."

"They're not hippies, Ruth," her father said. "They're just a group of people who live an *alternative lifestyle*." He over-enunciated his final two words.

"Are we supposed to stay away from them?" Miriam said.

"I don't think so," their father said. "We just wanted you to know in case you ever happened to see them."

"They live in cabins, we heard," their mother said. "Not right here by us, but on the other side of the woods." She pointed vaguely to the window and then returned to eating.

Zack was riveted. Ann had mentioned she lived on the other side of the woods.

"You good, Z?" Ethan said, and Zack looked up to see the others gazing at him. He hated when everyone had their eyes on him. All he really wanted was to be treated normally, the way things had been a year ago, and, before that, for all the years of his life.

"I'm good," he said, standing. "I think I'm gonna go to my room and read."

"You sure you don't want to stay here with us?" his father said.

"I'm sure," Zack said, heading for the stairs. "I just want to read."

What he really wanted, he thought, was for Susan to walk into the room and start talking and laughing. Just the way things used to be.

And he wanted to see Ann again.

— *Five* —

LIGHTS ACROSS THE RIVER

The next day was long and slow and hot, and Zack spent much of it in his room finishing *Falcons and Bandits* and then starting on its sequel, *Falcondale*, which he'd also read before. He loved the Falcons and Bandits series, all twelve of the books, mostly because the brothers and sisters in the stories were so plucky and imaginative, but also because their adventures—boating and camping and hiking—seemed like endless fun. It struck him that he now lived in a place where the exploits of the kids in the books were things he could do himself. It also hadn't escaped him that there were two brothers and three sisters in the books—just like his family.

Aside from the pleasure Zack found in his reading, though, and despite his preference to keep to himself, he had another reason for staying in his room for so many hours that day: He wanted to catch a glimpse of Ann. All morning and afternoon as Zack read on his bed, he kept an eye out for her, hoping to see her steal out of the woods and, maybe, return to the Tower or even visit the house. When nothing of the sort happened, Zack resigned himself to a quiet evening. Maybe he and Ethan would play backgammon, or Ruth would share some drawings with him, or his mother would make one of her famous blueberry pies.

It was after dinner and just when the sky was darkening that Ethan knocked on Zack's door and, upon entering, said, "We're going to the Tower, Z, the three of us, to look at the stars. You should come."

Ten minutes later, Ethan, Miriam, Ruth, and Zack were sitting on the steps of the Tower and admiring the night sky, which was steadily blackening. The stars here were much brighter and far more abundant than they'd ever been in Roseburg, a fact that delighted Zack. He'd seen the night sky like this before on camping trips or when the family had gone to the ocean, and he'd admired the stars every night since arriving earlier in the week. But the sight was as thrilling as ever. Out here, the dense spray of twinkling yellow was so entire that it felt endless, a riot of light across the black.

"If you follow the two stars on the lower side of the Big Dipper," Ethan said, pointing as he stood beside Zack, "and go straight out and down from them, you come to the North Star. Right there. And if you go up from it, you can see how it's part of the Little Dipper."

Zack not only admired his big brother, he was forever impressed by how much Ethan knew about the world around him. Ethan had been in Boy Scouts in Roseburg, and one of the first things he wanted to do once the family settled in at Vista Point was to find a new troop to join.

"You're eleven now, Z," Ethan had told him on several occasions over the past few months. "You're eligible to join up, too."

It sounded appealing, and Zack loved the thought of being able to venture out with Ethan on hikes and bicycle trips, just as his brother had done with his troop in Roseburg; but Zack hadn't yet committed to actually signing up for anything.

"The stars here are incredible," Ruth said, scanning the sky. "It makes you think about all the wishes people make on them."

"Don't tell me," Miriam said playfully. "There's a good story you could write about that?" She gestured upward. "What's that one called again, Ethan? The one that looks like a *W*?"

"Cassiopeia," Ethan said. "Down from the North Star. She was a queen. She's supposed to be holding a mirror there, but you have to use your imagination."

"*Cassiopeia looked at herself in her mirror and wondered if anyone would ever fall in love with her,*" Ruth said.

"You just do that to annoy us," Miriam said, and Ruth began to laugh with her and Ethan.

"I like your idea about fixing this place up, Zack," Ruth said. She stood and put a hand against the stone wall. "Seriously, I think we should do it. People would love to visit this old building." She was silent for a moment. "You guys like Vista Point so far? I miss my friends, but I have to admit, it's pretty cool out here. Peaceful. It's weird how quiet it is, but in a good way."

"I'm a little nervous about school," Ethan said. "Starting at a new place as a junior. I wanted to graduate in Roseburg, but, you know, we're here now, and Mom and Dad are excited about the bed-and-breakfast. And it's really cool being in the forest and above the river. Like camping, kind of."

"I know what you mean," Miriam said. "I could get used to living out here." This surprised Zack because, of all of them, Miriam was the most attached to city life. She loved to play basketball at the park near their house in Roseburg, and she spent large portions of the school year practicing or playing in the gym because she was the point guard on her team.

"Mom and Dad are really trying to make everything perfect for us," Ruth said.

"It is nice here," Zack said. Once again, there was that odd, fraught silence where everyone seemed both surprised and indulgent— maybe a little amazed, even—that Zack had spoken. "But our house was where Susan was," he added. "Where we all were."

Silence fell over the four of them once more. Even though crickets were chirping on all sides, Zack found himself sensing the quiet hum of the night—from the slight breeze, perhaps, or maybe from the slow press of water in the river far off. There was a small vibration in the air.

"I just feel like we're here now," Ethan said, "so I'm going to be positive about it."

"*Ethan Einstein, one of the most sensitive Boy Scouts to ever join Troop 213*," Ruth said.

"Aaahh!" Miriam growled. "Stop that!"

"Hey, what's that?" Ruth said abruptly. A peculiar and urgent note in her voice caused the others to freeze. The way she spoke made Zack think she'd heard a noise nearby, and for a split second the crazy thought came to him that Ann was approaching and had, perhaps, made a sound. But when he turned to look at his sister, she was peering directly across the river, far into the blackness of the opposite side. He looked, too. There, from within the dense bulk of shadow that rose up from the river on the northern shore—where there were only trees and where, even during the day, it was almost impossible to see any houses or roads—a light flashed.

"What?" Miriam said.

"Look there!" Ethan said, standing. He took a step and pointed. "A light flashing."

"Oh yeah," Miriam said. "Hey! I see it."

"Is that a car?" Ruth said.

"It's over half a mile to the other side from here, and that's a really bright light," Ethan said. "If it was a car, its lights would have to be really strong and facing perfectly straight at us."

"Then why is someone flashing a light like that?" Miriam said.

"No idea," Ethan answered.

The flickering continued as the four kids watched. There were a few faint, scattered lights among the stretch of blackness on the far side, from houses tucked away in the trees or some utility lamps along the unseen road there. But the opposite side of the Grand River from Vista Point was basically a single wall of shadow—and now a conspicuously bright light was flashing.

"What do you think it is?" Zack said. As he spoke the words, an incident from one of his books came to him. "Hey, you know what? In the fourth Falcons and Bandits book, the kids contact these other kids by flashing lights at them. Maybe it's something like that."

Ethan slapped his hand to his forehead with a loud smack. "You're a genius, Z! I should have known right off. That's Morse code, I'm positive. We learned about it at camp last year."

"Morse code, like dot-dash dot-dash and all that?" Miriam said.

"Yeah," Ethan said. "You signal the letters, and they add up to words. A quick flash is a dot, and when they hold the light a little longer, that's a dash."

"And then a message!" Ruth said. "Someone's sending us a message! It's like a story!"

"Wait, wait, wait," Miriam said. "It's dark out. No one knows we're here, and why would anyone send a message, anyway? It's just a coincidence." She paused. "Maybe it's not even Morse code. Maybe someone's superbright flashlight is freaking out."

"That looks extremely deliberate," Ethan said. "Oh man, I wish I had a piece of paper so I could write this down."

Zack turned to Ruth. "You didn't bring your journal?"

She shrugged as if to indicate the question made no sense, even though she was in the habit of keeping a small notebook with her most of the time in case some inspiration for a story or poem came to her. "When it's dark out?" Ruth said. "How could I write anything?"

"Let's try to remember what the flashes are," Ethan said, but just then the light blinked out. It had lasted three minutes at most, but now there was only blackness once more. The four kids waited for the light to resume—they were so eager to have it start back up that they were each mentally willing it to begin again, but after nearly a minute of waiting, it seemed all had ended.

"Let there be light!" Miriam yelled. She turned to Ethan, who was staring at her.

"That's sacrilegious, you know," Ethan said.

"Why do you use those big words all the time?" Miriam said.

"You, future flunker of her college entrance exam," Ethan said. "How Miriam—"

"Enough!" Ruth interrupted. "That was so cool, what we just saw. A message! A coded message!"

Zack looked to his brother. "Do you really think that's what it was?"

"I do," Ethan said. "I don't know what else it could be."

"But if someone's way over there flashing lights at ten o'clock at night," Miriam said, "they would be trying to communicate with someone over here, and that makes no sense. Why not just pick up the phone? Or drive over here?"

"Well," Ruth said, "maybe they were signaling to someone…" She turned to one side and then the other, as if she might catch a glimpse of a person way off in the darkness somewhere on their side of the river. "I don't know, like someone who lives near us. Who doesn't have a phone. Or…I don't know!"

"That light was more like a beam, I think," Ethan said. "Aiming right up here."

"Makes no sense," Miriam said. "I think it was just a fluky thing. Oh, gosh, I sound like Mom. *Fluky thing.*"

"We gotta tell Mom and Dad about this," Ethan said.

"Or we could keep it our secret," Ruth said. "More mysterious that way."

Zack took a few steps forward, closer to the edge of the bluff, and he stared into the blackness. The buzzing sound came to him, some sensation from the forest and the black sky and the river below. For a moment he felt certain the light would start up again.

"What if someone's looking for someone else?" he said. "A person who's lost?"

Silence.

Zack continued to stare across the river. "That was a message," he said. "I know it was."

"We should go inside," Ethan said. "We don't want Mom and Dad to worry."

"We need to come here tomorrow night," Miriam said. "We need to see if someone flashes those lights again."

Six

ANOTHER VISIT TO THE TOWER

Even after the four kids explained everything to their parents, no one could make heads or tails of the flashing lights, despite much conversation and speculation over the next few days. Ethan, Ruth, and Zack were certain someone had been attempting to send a message by using Morse code; Miriam and their father thought the lights were most likely just some sort of flickering from a car or house and that the blinking only appeared to be a deliberate signal; and their mother believed the whole thing was just a prank.

"Almost no one even knows we moved here," she said, "and why in the world would anyone think the four of you—or anyone— would be at the Tower at that time of night exactly? It was just some kids goofing around."

Ethan, though, spent part of the afternoon the day after the incident scanning the far side of the river with binoculars in an attempt to locate the spot from which the light had originated.

"I didn't see anything," he informed the family at dinner that night. "Just forest over there. I know there are some houses, because you can see a few lights at night. But during the day, the trees are too thick to make out almost anything at all."

"We'll go out with you tonight," their father said. "Once it gets dark."

No flashing lights appeared that night, however, even though the six Einsteins waited by the Tower until nearly eleven o'clock; and then nothing was seen the next night or the night after that. By Thursday, everyone was beginning to feel that the lights had been something strange and exciting but that there most likely wouldn't be any repeat of them—or any way of figuring out who had been behind them.

Besides, there was too much else to think about and do. On each weekday, a crew of three men their parents had hired—and who had been fixing up the mansion since April—arrived early in the morning and began working on the house and the surrounding property: patching the roof, replacing the gutters, cleaning and painting the siding, replacing the crumbling brickwork on the huge chimney, digging up parts of the yard to repair the septic tank and put in saplings, and doing a hundred other chores.

"Those three are lifesavers," their father would often say.

"And they're ahead of schedule," their mother would add. "A Labor Day opening is looking pretty good."

The four kids helped their parents on the less complicated work when and where they could—sanding the wooden floors in the hallways and bedrooms, helping their father replace trim and moldings, joining their mother in painting the walls inside. And there were furnishings to buy—beds and bureaus and bookcases and chairs—which meant an outing to Thornton Falls on the Tuesday after the lights had been flashing and then a drive to Roseburg (with a little side trip by their former house) to pick up a few things from a big store that sold appliances. On each day that week, as well, a truck or two arrived to deliver some large piece of furniture or packages of supplies for the kitchen. It was all very busy and very exhausting, and even Zack left his room for stretches to pitch in, though his contributions were minor compared with the others'. He just didn't feel much like doing anything besides remaining in his room; and if he wasn't reading, he was drawing superheroes in his art book or making things out of Legos, even though he sometimes wondered if he was getting too old for them. All the while, whether at his desk or lying on his bed, he kept an eye out for Ann, though he didn't see her emerge from the trees or make her way to the Tower—until Friday afternoon, one week exactly from when he'd seen her before.

He was reading on his bed once again when he saw her step out of the woods and—with frequent glances toward the house, as though hoping Zack would see her—head toward the Tower. Only his father and Ruth were at home (the others had gone to Thornton Falls), though Ruth was writing in her room and his father was putting in trim in one of the guest rooms. Zack headed to the hallway and was just out his bedroom door when a thought came to him—he tore a page from his notebook and put a piece of paper and a small pencil in his pocket. Downstairs he told his father, as nonchalantly as he could, that he was going outside for a little while; and then he stepped out the back door and began running toward the Tower. When he was halfway across the big field that lay between his house and the stone building, he saw the flash of a red T-shirt beside the Tower, and then Ann was waving at him. Zack waved in return as he trotted toward her.

"Hey," he said as he approached, breathing heavily. "You came back."

"I told you I would!" she said. "Like we agreed. I couldn't come for a long time, even though I wanted to."

Zack stopped before her. "Yeah, I kept looking for you."

The two of them were out of sight of the Einsteins' house, hidden by the Tower itself. Once again, Zack had the sensation of being much farther away from his house than he was—that he and Ann were alone and very distant from anyone else, from any place else.

She turned to gaze toward the field. "Your house looks beautiful from here."

"It's getting fixed up. My parents are always working on it. We all help out a little bit, my sisters and my brother. Me too."

"It's pretty huge," she said. "Way huger than mine."

"You know, we hike around on the trails here all the time. Maybe we could come by your house sometime. If it's okay."

"Sure," Ann said brightly. "I'll ask my mom." She smiled and then pointed to the Tower. "Want to go inside again?"

It was, in fact, just what Zack wanted to do, though he had no idea if the doors would be unlocked, and he continued to feel apprehensive about not abiding by his parents' rules. Still, he told himself, if their concern was that it might be dangerous to enter the Tower, Zack already knew that wasn't anything to worry about, given his earlier visit inside. He didn't like violating his parents' trust, but he was so eager to take another peek—and to see the medallion again—that he told himself it would be all right if he and Ann crept in.

"Yeah, I do," he said. "If it's open."

Ann put a funny look of uncertainty on her face, and said, "It better be!" Her words had come out so amusingly, the two of them began giggling.

Zack looked up at the Tower, which seemed both graceful and sturdy, with its gray stone walls and delicate columns at each point of its nine sides. It looked immense and mysterious—Zack had the strangest sensation of the Tower beckoning him inside.

"It's such a cool building," he said, turning to Ann, who was gazing at it with her mouth open. "We've even been talking about fixing it up maybe someday. So people can visit it whenever. We'd have to buy it first, but still."

Ann seemed almost not to hear him. She moved to the stairs and stepped up them toward the door; and then, when she reached the small terrace atop the steps, she turned to face Zack. She waved at him even though he was only a few feet away, and then she shifted her gaze to take in the river far below and the mountains in the distance and the broad swath of green forest across the Grand River. Zack watched her.

"You can see everything from right here," she said. She looked up and down the river in both directions for a moment, and then she returned her eyes to the dense forest directly opposite the Tower on the northern side of the silently flowing river. She pressed her face forward just slightly and squinted as if attempting to spot something. For a moment, Zack had the feeling that Ann was looking somewhere in the area where he and his siblings had seen the flashing lights. She kept her gaze fixed and continued to stare across the river.

"What do you see?" Zack said after a moment.

Her concentration broke; Ann smiled and lifted both arms into a huge shrug. "Everything!" she said, and then she turned to the doors, grabbed the handle of one, and gave a hard tug. The door creaked, and Ann whipped her head around to look at Zack.

"It's open!" she said.

A moment later, the two of them were standing at the exact center of the broad marble floor, surrounded by a diffuse green and gold light and staring up at the ceiling. To Zack, the inside of the Tower felt just as peaceful and shadowy and still as it had when he'd visited it the previous time with Ann. The medallion glinted high above, and the circle of plaques—the nine stone faces along the rim of the second level—seemed to stare silently across the vast open space above. Zack turned to Ann, who continued to gaze upward.

"I started wondering if maybe you couldn't come back to see me," Zack said.

Ann shook her head. "I don't get to go out a lot. Just sometimes. My mother's a waitress in a restaurant down on the highway." She pointed toward the door behind them, and Zack understood she was indicating the road that skirted the river.

"A lot of times she takes me with her, and I draw or read while she's working," Ann said. "And she gives me a piece of blackberry pie and vanilla ice cream. It's so good! And there's a trail to Silver Chute Falls—you've been there, probably—so I walk up there, and there's lots of people around. When she doesn't work, I get to explore all around here. And sometimes she lets me stay home on my own, but not that much."

"Where do you go to school?"

"Vista Point Elementary. I'm going into fifth grade."

Zack didn't realize there was an elementary school near their house; he and his siblings were going to be taking the bus to Thornton Falls for school when September arrived, and he thought he'd heard his mother mention that there weren't any schools nearby, though perhaps she hadn't been thinking of schools for younger kids.

"I thought the only elementary school was in Thornton Falls," Zack said.

"No, I've been going to Vista Point Elementary since kindergarten. My teacher this coming year is going to be Miss Black. She's the better one of the fifth-grade teachers, everyone says, so I'm glad I get to have her. The other one is Mrs. Vlah, and all the kids say she's really mean. She writes your name on the board if you talk too much, and she looks funny."

Zack studied Ann as she returned her gaze to the ceiling high above. "You and my little sister have a birthday around the same time."

Ann looked at him. "The one who had the accident?"

"Yeah."

"What happened to her?"

"We were at a fair last summer, and she ran after a kitten. That's when the accident happened. With a car."

"Was it bad?"

There was a notion in Zack's head that kept trying to find an end, that seemed close to coming together; but just as he always did when this feeling arose, he cut the thought off before it went too far.

"She's gone," he said, almost whispering the words, though he didn't know what he wanted to say next.

"What was her name?" Ann said.

"Susan."

"Did you all do a lot of things together?"

Zack considered where to start. There were days where most of his thoughts centered on Susan or returned to Susan, no matter what he was doing or what else he was thinking about. But now that Ann was asking him about what they did, he couldn't figure out what to say.

"We used to watch cartoons together on the couch," he said finally. "On Saturday. She would kind of rest on the couch right next to me. She liked to ask a lot of questions, and sometimes even the things that weren't scary would kind of scare her. At least, they weren't really what you would think of as scary things. She would hold my hand."

He stopped talking.

"You must really miss her," Ann said. "Like my father. I haven't seen him in a long time, either."

"Why not?"

"He died in the war." She hesitated before adding: "He was a soldier."

It took Zack a second or two to register the words. He knew

there was news sometimes—online or in the *Roseburg Journal*, which his parents liked to read—about wars and how there was fighting going on in some parts of the world. But all that seemed very far away. He'd never known anyone—as far as he was aware—whose father was an actual soldier, much less who'd been killed fighting. The word *died*—so stark and final—made almost no sense to him when he heard it come out of Ann's mouth. The way she'd said it made it seem both ordinary and distant, as though it described something that had happened to a person she didn't know. He couldn't picture uttering the word himself.

"In the war?" Zack said. *Which war?* he wanted to add.

Ann nodded. "Yes, in the war. So it's just the two of us now." She tugged at her ponytail.

"Did it happen a while ago?" he said.

She nodded. "About a year ago."

That didn't seem like a very long time to Zack, but before he could say anything in response, Ann continued to speak. "At first I didn't really think it happened," she said. "My mother told me about it, but I didn't…I don't know. I didn't think he was really dead, I guess."

Neither of them spoke for a moment. Zack wasn't sure what to say, and he had the feeling Ann didn't want to talk about her father any more than he wanted to talk about Susan. He pointed up at the medallion.

"Let's go back to where we were so we can look at that silver thing again," he said.

They moved to the stairs and scrambled up to the second level before moving to the spot along the walkway where the medallion was easiest to see in the light.

"They're not real words," Zack said, peering at the silver disk. "It's just a bunch of jumbled-up letters."

"It doesn't make any sense," Ann said.

He pointed upward. "But there's one capital letter on each line. I did notice that."

Zack removed the paper and pencil from his pocket and then spread the paper out and pressed it flat against the top of the railing.

"That's a good idea," Ann said. "I wish I'd thought of that." She leaned closer to the paper as Zack wrote, glanced up, wrote some more, and on and on until he'd copied the three lines and the words at the center of the medallion, *One of Nine.*

"Could you write that out for me, too?" Ann said.

"Yeah. That's no problem."

"I want to take it home."

Zack tore off the bottom half of his page and wrote the lines, then presented it to Ann.

"Thanks," she said, and she folded the paper and started to put it in her pocket before unfolding it and examining the lines. "Do you think it's a secret message?"

"I don't know," he said. "But that would be so cool if it was."

"Have you ever read a book called *Falcons and Bandits*?"

"Read it?" Zack said, his voice so loud that it echoed through the Tower in a tremor of vibration. "It's my favorite."

"Mine, too," Ann said. "I've read all the books. Well, not all, but about half of them."

"I've read all of them a few times. You know, there's five Falcons. Just like in my family."

"I like the Bandits the best. The two sisters. They can do everything, like sailing and hiking and all of it." She smiled, showing Zack her slightly crooked teeth again. "But I was thinking how the kids find a secret message in the second book." She pointed to the medallion. "So maybe it's just like that."

"Let's figure it out," Zack said. "I can work on it at home. See if there's a code or something."

Ann held out a hand to shake. "So will I. We can be like one Falcon and one Bandit!"

Zack laughed. "Okay!"

They became silent once again, and Zack gazed at the medallion high above. As he stood looking, he felt the hint of a faint breeze on his face, something soothing and cool. A thought came to him of Susan, and he stood with the feeling of gentle air on his skin for a moment. He put a hand to his cheek and turned to Ann, who was looking at him.

"Did you feel that?" he said softly just as the breeze ended; and she nodded, her eyebrows lowering quizzically.

"Like a little wind," she said.

"Yeah." Zack studied the windows along the second level; the ones that weren't boarded up were unbroken. "That's strange," he said. "I wonder where it came from."

"The door, I guess," Ann said, though Zack thought that was unlikely. The breeze had felt so gentle, less a pressing against his skin than a light touch.

Ann smiled at him. "Hey, can I show you something outside? A place I know about?"

"Is it far?" Zack said. He wondered how long it would be until his father started calling for him.

"Just down the hill a little bit," Ann said. "Come on."

Seven

THE CAVE ON THE HILL

Five minutes later, after stepping back out into the sunshine and closing the Tower's doors behind them and then traipsing down the bluff about a hundred yards and a bit to the west, Ann stopped amid a stand of cedars on a broad flat patch.

"Look at this," she said, pointing to what looked to Zack like part of a fallen tree—and then he realized it was an enormous stump, at least ten feet in diameter.

"That's huge," he said. "That tree must have been gigantic." He looked up into the sky as if to visualize what the tree must have looked like, and then he jumped onto the flattest portion of the stump and paced it off.

"My father told me there used to be these really tall trees everywhere here," Ann said. "This is the biggest stump I've found. Actually, my father showed it to me."

"You two must have hiked all around here."

"I remember where it was because this is such a neat spot."

Zack had never heard anyone his age use the word *neat*. He thought there was something old-fashioned about the word, but he liked the way Ann had said it.

"Neat?" Zack said. "How?"

She looked past him and toward a steep portion of the hillside close to them; and then she put her hand beside her face and pointed forward next to her eye, as if sighting a distant speck of an island from a boat.

"Because if you find this stump," she said, "then you can find the cave that's here." She moved her finger straight ahead. "Right there."

Zack turned to see a depression in the side of the hill that looked like a dip in the brush, and then Ann dashed off straight for it, and he followed; when she arrived, she swept an overhang of moss-encrusted roots and grass to reveal a small cave, maybe five feet high and about six feet deep into the rock.

"Whoa!" Zack said. "A hidden cave!" He looked to Ann with wide eyes.

"I know. My father showed it to me. He said to be careful in case there was something in here, like an animal, I guess." She peered into the obviously empty rock depression. "But there's nothing here that I can see."

"Me neither," Zack said, examining the space with wonder as he lifted his arm to press more of the obscuring brush aside. "Let's go in."

The two of them stepped within, and then Zack slowly dropped his arm so that the front of the cave was mostly covered once more. It wasn't all that dark inside, but he felt as though the two of them were at least as hidden as they'd been inside the Tower, and the smell of soil and grass made Zack feel he was both outside and inside all at the same time.

"This is too cool," he said, looking around. "Definitely like *Falcons and Bandits*! You came here with your father?"

"We used to," Ann said.

"Hey, look here!" Zack said, pointing to a spot at the very rear of the cave and just level with his head. "Someone carved something."

Ann stood beside Zack and examined the rock wall. There was just enough light to see a string of letters, no more than an inch tall, faintly carved into the smooth sandstone: *Always yours, Jing. Ray.*

"Ray?" Zack said. "And Jing? What does all that mean?"

"I don't know," Ann said. "But look under it, too. I see more."

Zack scanned downward a half foot and saw another line, even more faintly carved: *Ray, I'm sorry I lost you.*

"*Ray* again," Zack said.

Ann gazed at the lines. "I wonder who wrote those things here." She reached out a hand to run her fingers over the rock. "It's... interesting."

"It must have taken the person a long time to carve it." Zack looked at Ann. "Ray and Jing. I wonder who they are."

"We should try to find out," Ann said, her eyes brightening. She looked toward the covered entrance of the cave as if she'd heard something. "But I don't know how."

Zack extended his arms wide, nearly touching both sides of the cave at once.

"Is it okay if I show my brother and sisters this place?" he said, and then he instantly thought better of it. "Or maybe it should be our own place. If you want."

"Yeah!" Ann said. "Falcons and Bandits! Our secret." She moved forward and, as seemed to be her habit, extended a hand to Zack to shake on it.

"Our secret," he said. "Hey, I have an idea, too. Maybe we could leave notes for each other here, like for when we can meet up and stuff like that."

"I like that," Ann said. "Let's do it. It can be part of the secret." She pointed to the ground. "Let's sit down."

"Your mother really doesn't mind if you go out in the woods all alone?" Zack said once they were seated.

"She says it's okay as long as I don't go off the main trails and as long as I'm not gone too long."

Zack couldn't imagine his parents letting him wander through the woods on his own, and he was two years older than Ann.

"It must be pretty safe here," he said. "In Roseburg, I always had to be with either Ethan or Miriam if I was away from the house. They're the two oldest."

"I think it's safe here. That's what my mother says, too." She began running a finger over the hard soil beside her leg. "Every once in a while, I get a little scared when I'm by myself in the forest if it's really quiet and there are a lot of trees so it's not so sunny. Did you ever read 'Hansel and Gretel'?"

"Yeah. Where the kids end up at the witch's house?"

"That's right. I remember when we read that in school, and then sometimes I would be out here walking and I would think about that story and where the witch lived." Ann widened her eyes. "It was scary!"

"Have you ever seen the people who live out in the woods?" Zack was trying to recall what his mother and father had said at dinner the week before. *The other side of the woods*, he remembered. *They live in cabins.* He recalled, too, that Ann had said she lived in the same area.

"Lots of people live in the woods," she said. "There are plenty of houses here."

"My parents said there's, like, a camp of people in a bunch of cabins somewhere. Not like regular houses."

"People in a bunch of cabins?" Ann said. "I haven't seen anything like that."

Something in the way she spoke and the pensive way she was sitting made Zack wonder if maybe she was concealing something. He knew it would seem odd if he pressed her, but he had a funny feeling that perhaps she really did know about the people in the woods and just didn't want to tell him about them. Or, he thought, maybe she herself lived there with them.

"What's your house like?" Zack found himself asking.

"Just a regular house," Ann said with a shrug. "I don't know. Just regular. Not too big."

He was about to ask her another question, but she seemed uncomfortable suddenly, so he decided to stop.

"My brother and sisters and I have been exploring around here," Zack said. "Not a whole lot yet, but we want to see the area, all the trails. You should come with us sometime. They would really like you, I know it."

"I'll try," she said, though she didn't sound too excited. "That would be fun."

"I'm just hanging out most of the time. You could even come to our house if you want."

"And we could meet at the stone building, too," Ann said.

That seemed such an odd way of sidestepping his invitation, Zack thought. He couldn't figure out why she seemed so intent on fending him off all of a sudden.

"The Tower," he said. "That's what we call the stone building."

"The Tower! I like that. I'll call it that, too."

"Another deal," Zack said.

Ann laughed finally. "Yes, another deal."

"Hey," he said, "I'll leave a note here for you in a day or two, okay? And you can come and find it and write one back to me. Or if you come here first, you can leave one for me and I'll answer it."

"Deal!" Ann said, sounding even more chipper now. "I'll do it." She extended a hand to Zack, and they shook once again.

"I'd better get going," he said, standing. "My dad will start wondering where I went." Ann remained sitting. "You want to walk back that way with me?"

"I think I'll stay here for a little bit," she said. "It's so peaceful. I'm just going to sit and think."

Zack gave a small laugh. "Okay. Well, don't think too hard. You don't want to miss out on any pie and ice cream your mother has waiting for you."

Now it was Ann's turn to laugh. "I won't. I'm just going to stay for a few minutes."

As Zack scanned the cave again, his eyes landed on the carvings on the wall.

"Hey, Ann," he said, pointing to the lines. "You never saw those words before when you came here?"

She shook her head. "Never."

How can that be? he thought. He examined the lines once more. They weren't carved too deeply into the rock, and they were a bit hard to see in the dull light, but they stood out easily enough. Even someone who wasn't looking carefully would most likely have noticed them after a few minutes in the cave.

"They look like they've been here a long time," Zack said. "Don't you think?"

"I can't really tell. This is the first time I've seen them." She shrugged. "I like the note idea. A lot. I won't tell anyone about this place, either. Our secret."

"I won't, either," Zack said. "Our secret."

Secret. It was the word that remained echoing in his head the rest of the afternoon, all the more so because—as glad as he'd been to see Ann a second time—he felt certain there was some secret she was keeping from him.

— *Eight* —

SWIMMING AT THE
WATERFALL

Y ou four don't have to help us all day, you know," their father
told the kids the next afternoon following lunch. "Go out and
have some fun."

Which is exactly what they did. There were trails heading off
into the forest on either side of the house—east and west—and the
Einstein kids were eager to follow all of them and find out where
they led. They'd already taken a few short hikes—Zack included,
on about half of them—to get their bearings in the area. As it
turned out, almost all the trails wound through the dense stands of
cedar and fir and hemlock and arrived at little natural pools in the
forest or—just as good—waterfalls, because Vista Point was right
between the mountains to the south and the Grand River. In fact,

the entire area was famous for its waterfalls, and the highway paralleling the river had all sorts of spurs up into the miles-long bluff that allowed drivers to enjoy the multitude of waterfalls slicing through the hills. Some of the spots—famous Silver Chute Falls and Angel Veil Falls and Weeping Stone Falls—had large parking lots and paved trails, and they drew scores of visitors almost every day, at least during the summer. The Einsteins had visited all of these falls before on their drives over the years and were familiar with the better-known spots. Now, though, the four kids wanted to discover the out-of-the-way falls, the ones very few people saw and almost no one visited.

"There are waterfalls everywhere around here," Ethan marveled as, on a trail a mile east of their house the day after Ann had shown Zack the cave, three good-sized tumbles of water were visible on the ledge above them. He, Zack, and the girls had been out for an hour; they were continuing to become more familiar with the woods. It had been a week since they'd seen the flashing lights, and now the thing of most interest to them was the intricate network of water that flowed, almost unseen through the lush green of the forest, all around them as it sought the enormous river below.

"That looks like a good little place to wade," Miriam said, pointing ahead to a clearing where the water had settled into a small natural pool before trickling away on the far side. When they arrived, they discovered that it was more than just a good spot to wade—because of a cluster of boulders that lay at the edge of the

65

slope and served as a sort of dam, the pool of water was waist-deep and a good ten feet across.

"We can actually swim here!" Ruth said, and within two minutes, she, Miriam, and Ethan had pulled off their shoes and the shorts and shirts they were wearing over their swimsuits, and were splashing around.

"Come in, Zack!" Miriam called. "The water's wet!"

He smiled at her old joke but waved her off and took a spot on a rock beside a couple of alders. As the three others kicked around in the water and ducked under to see how long they could hold their breath, Zack examined the clearing. He pictured himself coming here often; it was so simple and beautiful—the kind of place Susan would have loved.

The gentle waterfall on the slope behind him—more of a thin seep of water down the rocks—was twenty feet high at most, and the incline was gradual. It looked to Zack as if there would be no difficulty in scrambling up the dirt and brush patch beside the rocks to see what lay above.

"I'll be right back," he called to the others, pointing up to the top of the falls. "I'm gonna check out what's up there."

"Just go on top," Ethan called, wiping the water from his face as he stood to answer his brother. He glanced toward where Zack was pointing. "Don't go anywhere else, okay?"

"I won't." Zack looked at the others—they had stopped to look at him, and for one awkward moment things got too quiet, too still.

"Don't worry," Zack added.

He turned and began half stepping and half clambering up the incline, and he was glad to hear his siblings resume their frolicking below. With a few quick pushes and lifts, Zack reached the level ground above and found himself even more amazed by the clearing here than the one he and his siblings had just discovered: a natural pool at least three times as broad as the one below lay spread before him, rimmed by tall alders that arched high over the water, almost like a dome. It was so dramatic and unexpected, Zack felt delighted, and he stood taking it all in and, especially, admiring the trees above.

He looked down at his brother and sisters in the water.

"It's cool up here," he called. "There's another place to go swimming. It's even bigger than where you guys are."

"You should come back down," Ruth called.

"One sec," Zack said, and he moved off to the side of the pool and out of sight of the others. The area around the water was very quiet and very dim, with thick ferns covering the ground beneath the high trees; Zack looked up, felt the silence around him.

Something moved at the edge of his vision. He spotted a Steller's jay arcing from some hidden spot and onto the branch of a cedar tree in the darker part of the woods, maybe fifty feet from the water. It sat examining the forest with quick, jerking glances. Zack loved the color of these birds—the lustrous blue of their bodies and the deeper blue-black of their crested heads—even though he'd seen them become cawing annoyances when he and his family had gone camping. He took a few cautious steps in the bird's direction, and it flew off. Behind the tree, just beyond a stand of alders, Zack thought he noticed something that looked vaguely squarish in shape, though it was so indistinct, he couldn't be sure. He took another step forward, keeping his eye on the spot.

"Hey, Z!" came Ethan's voice behind him, and Zack turned to see his brother—in his wet swimming trunks and with his tennis shoes on—emerging over the ledge at the end of the broad pool. "Look at this place!"

Miriam and Ruth, their suits dripping with water, were right behind him; and they, too, went wide-eyed when they saw the clearing Zack had discovered. Zack peered back in the direction he'd been heading but decided, without knowing why, to say nothing to his siblings—at least for the moment.

"Incredible!" Ruth said. "Now, *this* is the kind of place you could write a story about."

"Good job, Zack," Miriam said. "Best spot so far."

"Our secret place!" Ruth said.

Ethan came to him and extended a clenched fist for Zack to tap. "Seriously nice job," he said. "You're like an honorary Boy Scout already." Ethan peered down at the water and then looked to his sisters. "As deep as the other one. Maybe deeper."

"You gotta swim here, Zack," Miriam said. "No getting out of it this time."

And five minutes later, after Zack had stripped down to his shorts and was splashing around in the water with the others, he couldn't help thinking what a great spot they'd chanced upon and how much he was enjoying the day.

"*The valiant brothers and sisters spent an invigorating afternoon soaking in the famous mineral baths near Einstein Manor,*" Ruth said once the kids had had their fill of the water and were lounging in the sunny clearing.

"If you could just figure out some way to keep that stuff inside your head and not say it out loud," Miriam said, "the world would be a better place."

"Hey!" Ethan called with excitement. He was studying the ground near a cluster of boulders on the opposite side of the water and had plucked something off the dirt. "An arrowhead!"

"Let me see," Ruth said, and Ethan returned to the others to display a flattish black arrowhead two inches long, which they all examined.

"That's cool, Ethan," Miriam said. "Do you know what it's made of?"

"Obsidian, I'm almost sure," Ethan said. "It's really common around here. It's a volcanic kind of rock."

Zack peered at the arrowhead in his brother's palm with amazement. That someone had made it years before and that it had lain forgotten and unseen until just now—it all seemed magical to him, like finding a message in a bottle from long ago.

"I have a few of these in my collection already, Zack," Ethan said. "Why don't you keep this one? Or you could even start your own collection." He held the arrowhead out to his brother.

"Thanks," Zack said, taking the thing and looking at it more closely now as it sat in his own palm.

"Don't lose it, Zack," Miriam said with mock sternness. "That would be bad luck."

"For Z, that arrowhead will be good luck," Ethan said. "He won't lose it."

Zack closed his fingers around the arrowhead, though not tightly. "I'll keep it safe," he said, and he picked up his pants, put the arrowhead in a pocket, and rolled the pants up tightly.

"Do you think Mom and Dad want us home soon?" Ruth said, so tentatively that it made everyone pause. The four kids glanced at one another; it seemed no one wanted to be the first to say it was time to end their adventures for the day.

The silence moved Zack to point into the woods. "I think I noticed something over there," he said. "A little building or something, maybe."

Ethan's eyes went wide. "Let's check it out."

A few minutes later, once the kids had dried off and changed out of their swimsuits, they made their way through the trees in the direction Zack had indicated. There, in a spot that looked as if it had once been a small clearing but was now overgrown with alders, stood a small log cabin with moss in its crevices and on its roof, and with all its windows broken. The four kids stood before it in silence, solemnly studying the dilapidated cedar house.

"Wow," Miriam said quietly. "No one has lived here for a while, that's for sure."

Ruth took a step toward the cabin. "Can you imagine living here, so far away from everything?" She turned to look at the others. "You could just write all day!"

Miriam frowned. "It would be pretty lonely in this place."

"With the water close by and this being such a nice spot," Ethan

71

said, "I'm sort of surprised this cabin is abandoned. Or that no one lives right around here."

Zack put a hand in his pocket and ran his fingers over the arrowhead.

"Should we look inside?" he said.

"No," Ethan said immediately. "Not safe, and we don't know who this belongs to. We shouldn't go in there."

"But don't you want to see, at least?" Miriam said, and she moved to one of the broken windows and peered in. The others followed, though all they saw inside were pieces of rotted logs and some broken glass. Other than that, the single room of the cabin was empty.

"Messy!" Ruth said, backing away. "Come on. Let's get home."

"Yikes!" Miriam called suddenly as a Steller's jay—the one from before, Zack felt certain—swooped past her and landed on the roof of the cabin. It began bobbing and cawing, and Ethan broke into a huge laugh.

"That thing scared you, Mir!" he said.

"It tried to kill me!" Miriam said.

Ethan patted Zack on his shoulder. "Let's go, Z!" And he dashed past Zack back toward the water where'd they been swimming. Miriam and Ruth followed; and Zack, too, was about to begin running—but he took one last look at the cabin and saw the jay winging off into the trees.

Who lived here? he wondered. And as he turned to race after the others, he thought: *Maybe Ann knows.*

— *Nine* —

AN UNWELCOME VISIT

All six of the Einsteins went to Thornton Falls that evening to have dinner and watch a movie, and then, four days later—the day before the big Fourth of July celebration that was going to be held in a park a few miles up the road beside the river—their breakfast was disturbed by a loud banging on the front door of their house.

"Who's that?" their father said, mostly to himself. He, Deborah, and the kids were sitting around the dining room table enjoying the oatmeal, cinnamon bread, and boiled eggs Miriam had prepared. Ethan had been talking about the Scout troop in Thornton Falls he was considering joining; Miriam explained she'd met the basketball coach for the junior varsity team at the school she and Ethan would attend in September; and Ruth had been explaining why she preferred Emily Dickinson's poems to anyone else's, when the loud knocking shattered the morning's peace.

Their mother glanced out the large window on the far wall of the dining room; the three workers were spreading gravel on the parking strip that was being put in.

"That's not one of the crew," she said, pointing. "They're all right there working."

"They wouldn't be banging like that anyway," their father said as he rose and headed into the hallway toward the front door. "Let me see what's up."

The four kids remained at the table while their mother stood to follow their father. Zack listened as the door creaked open.

"Good morning," his father said to someone. "May I help you?"

"Are you Morton Einstein?" came a voice—a man's voice, very gruff and loud.

Ethan's eyes went wide, and he shot up from his seat just before the girls did the same. Zack followed suit, wondering who would be visiting this early and speaking so rudely to their father.

"I am he," his father said. "And whom do I have the pleasure of meeting this fine morning?"

Zack arrived in the hallway just in time to see the man—balding, with sparse white hair and glasses, and dressed in faded corduroy pants and a flannel shirt—move his eyes past their father to take in the sight before him: six Einsteins, the four kids in order behind their parents.

"Oh, there's a whole group of you," the man said, his tone even less generous than it had been already. He appeared to be close to seventy, Zack thought, and it was impossible to picture his grizzled face ever holding a smile. He seemed to Zack to resemble some of the men who drove the trucks that delivered things to their house, and he was tall enough to look down on Zack's father—and big enough, practically, to have rammed through the door if he'd not wanted to knock. Zack was glad to be the farthest one from him as he gaped at the man.

"I'm Deborah Einstein," Zack's mother said kindly, "and you've just now met my husband, Morton, and these are our children, Ethan, Miriam, Ruth, and Zack. If you're a neighbor, we're very pleased to meet you. Though even if you're not, you're welcome to our new home."

The man's face went momentarily blank even though he kept his unblinking eyes on Deborah, and then he began working his lips together briefly before saying, "Well, this *new home* of yours used to be mine, and I—"

"Wonderful!" Morton said, cutting him off. "There are a lot of questions we have for you about the place. Won't you come in, please?"

"I have no intention of coming in," the man said curtly, his scowl deepening. Zack had a feeling the man might grab his father—he looked so agitated. It was hard to imagine what he could be so angry about, but it was clear he'd arrived with something upsetting on his mind. "But I do have some news you'll want to hear, I guarantee you."

Silence. Everyone, the white-haired man included, seemed to hold their breath to see what would happen next.

"Share away, please," Morton said.

"This was *my* house a half dozen owners ago," the man said, jabbing a single finger toward the ground at his feet as if to make his point clear, "and this was my property. All of it. Taken— unlawfully—years ago. Now, it's bad enough that anyone would live on stolen property, but it's come to my attention that you intend—"

"Sir," Deborah interrupted, "I understand you have some sort of grievance, it appears, but it's not appropriate for you to just show up here and start haranguing us."

Zack looked past the man and saw the three workers drawing close to the house behind him. He felt relieved—if there was any trouble, the three men would be able to help them.

"Call it whatever you like," the man said acidly, "but I'm going to speak my piece, and you'll be glad I did. Let's just say I'm positive about that."

"Do you have a name, at least?" Morton said. "We don't even know who you are."

"Horatio Cuvallo," the man said grimly. "Everyone around here knows me." He pointed downward again. "And they know this is mine. The whole thing. Or should be. Now, you might have the law on your side when it comes to ownership of the place, but from what I've heard, you have plans to make this a little inn or something."

"A bed-and-breakfast," Ethan said. "The best one ever!"

His father turned to him and gave a nod. "Thanks, son. I'll handle this."

"Well," Horatio continued, his voice laced with sarcasm, "that sure sounds like a cute little plan, but I'm here to inform you it's illegal to run a business on this property. I may have had this place stolen from me, but I know the regulations, and I have the paperwork. No moneymaking venture can be set up here. No profiteering. It's a clear violation of county law."

"Mr. Cuvallo," Deborah said, "surely you don't think we've started in on our venture without researching the legality of it? It's clear you're upset about what's happened in the past, but we had nothing to do with that. And we're positive it's legal to move forward with our plans."

"Positive, are you?" Horatio said, pulling back his head and regarding Deborah with a mocking expression. "Completely positive? I find that very interesting, given the conversations I've been having with my friends at the county."

"I'm sure you have a lot of friends there," Morton said.

Zack felt a jolt go through him, some combination of pleasure at his father's biting words, but also a flash of fear that maybe he'd gone too far and the man would become doubly incensed.

Horatio Cuvallo straightened up and took a small half step forward. "I don't know if that's your attempt at being funny," he said, his voice quieter than it had been the whole time, "but just go ahead and keep joking around while your little bed-and-breakfast plans fall apart."

"You don't scare me, Mr. Cuvallo," Morton said. "And this is our property, and you need to get off it right now."

Several long seconds of silence once again followed, and then Horatio reached up to scratch his jaw.

"I fought in Vietnam for three years," he said, so softly it was difficult for Zack to hear him. "I was with the merchant marine for twenty, and I've hauled more freight around this country than you'll ever see in your lifetime. If you think a little pipsqueak like you from Roseburg is going to waltz in here and do whatever he likes on land that should be mine, you got another thing coming." He looked up from Morton to stare at the kids. "Enjoy your morning, folks," he said, and then he turned on his heels and stalked off, not glancing at the three men as he passed them.

The kids joined their mother and father in the doorway to watch Horatio get into his truck, back out with a skid on the dirt and gravel, and roar off down the lane toward the main road beyond the trees. No one spoke until he was gone. The three men headed back to their work.

"Some really nice people out here in the country," Deborah said.

"Deb," Morton said consolingly.

She looked to the kids. "That's actually the first bad apple we've come across out here."

"What was he talking about?" Ruth said. "We can't have our bed-and-breakfast place?"

"He's dead wrong there," their mother said. "Don't worry about that. Your father and I spent weeks looking into things."

"He sounded pretty certain," Miriam said.

"There are people like that in the world who want to intimidate you," their father said. "He's out of line. That's all there is to it."

"Maybe you should check in with someone at the county office," Ethan said.

"There's nothing to check," his father said. "Believe me, we had lawyers up and down on this deal. We're fine."

But Zack felt rattled by the whole thing—the interruption of the morning, Horatio's menacing words and his anger, the possibility that there might be trouble ahead, legal or otherwise. And there had been a passing comment Horatio had made, too, about fighting in a war. It was odd—Ann had explained that her father had been a soldier, and now this strange and angry man had appeared and mentioned he'd once been a soldier. There was no possible connection, certainly—Horatio was old enough to be Ann's grandfather, the war he'd been in was decades old, and, of course, he was alive. Still, the coincidence of it was strange, and Zack couldn't get the connection out of his head as he considered it over the rest of the morning.

Just before lunch, he slipped away to the cave beneath the Tower and left a note for Ann: *We're going to be at the Fourth of July festival at the park near Columbia Locks. I'll look for you!*

Zack had been hoping he might actually see Ann, if not near the Tower, then perhaps here at the cave, though he knew the odds of either were slim. Still, he felt disappointed that she didn't appear, and he lingered in the cave for several minutes waiting for her, almost willing her to arrive. In order to stretch the time out just a bit longer, Zack went to the wall at the rear of the cave and studied the lines there once again.

Always yours, Jing. Ray.

Ray, I'm sorry I lost you.

The second line seemed deeply sad to Zack, the sort of thing a person would write if they never expected to see someone again. Had the words been in answer to the first line, perhaps, a message two people had shared? There was, Zack felt, probably no way to figure any of it out.

As he gazed at the carved lines, he put a hand into his pocket and touched the arrowhead he kept there. He thought of Susan, pictured her reading the lines. A noise sounded outside the cave.

Zack dashed out and looked in all directions, frantic with excitement.

"Ann?" he called. But she wasn't there. The river was far below, and the clouds in the sky hovered as though they might never move.

"Ann?" Zack said, not as loudly this time. "Are you there?"

After a moment, he felt in his pocket for the arrowhead—just to make certain it was still there—and turned to walk up the hill to the big field so he could return home.

— *Ten* —

A CIRCLE OF TREES

Zack didn't see Ann at the Fourth of July celebration the next day, and when he returned to the cave the morning after the fireworks, his note was still there, untouched. He took it up from off the ground and stuffed it into his pocket.

The rest of the morning passed in typical fashion, with the Einstein kids pitching in on various chores and projects around the house. Miriam had a knack for hanging wallpaper, she was discovering, and Ruth was becoming an expert at staining the old bookcases and cabinets that had either come with the house or been delivered to it at their parents' request. Ethan was skilled at measuring and cutting the trim that needed replacing in nearly all the rooms, while Zack mainly just did whatever his mother or father asked of him—sanding some of the upstairs floors or scrubbing the tiles in the bathrooms. It wasn't much fun, he had to admit—he didn't seem to have the same enthusiasm for the work that his siblings had—but he was glad to help out, glad to see his parents happy with the progress of the place.

"I've been doing a little research on our house," their mother announced at lunch as everyone took a break from their work. "It wasn't always this big, huge place. It started off as just a regular little house, but then the people who had it—before the couple we bought it from—added rooms to make it into what it is now. The Vales—that was their name." She pointed to the kitchen and then the front door off the dining room hallway. "Before them, the house used to be pretty much just this area here."

Zack looked around and considered what his mother had explained as the others moved on to talk about the work ahead and what it would be like to have people actually stay in their house as guests. He was wondering why the owners all those years ago had decided to make the house so large, when something came to him that he hadn't thought of before.

"Do you think," he began, and everyone stopped talking because Zack's interruption had been so sudden, "we could go back to the fair again this year?"

His mother's face went slack. "The one we went to last summer?"

"Yeah," Zack said. As he looked to the faces of his brother and sisters, he felt a little drop in his stomach.

"Why do you want to go back there, Z?" Ruth said.

"I don't know," Zack said, and as he spoke the words, he recognized that he really didn't know why he wanted to return to the fair. "That's where Susan ran after that kitten, and…" He lost the thread of his thought. "I don't know. I just thought we could go there again."

His father set his fork down and sighed quietly. "Zack," he said with patient finality. "Susan was struck by a car. I know you understand that, as hard as it is."

"Dad," Miriam said softly, a note of pleading in her voice.

"No, really," their father said insistently but gently. "We're all going through this. Together. We loved her and we miss her terribly." He looked at Zack. "And I know how tough this has been on you. We've all experienced so many ups and downs." He took off his glasses and put the back of his wrist to his eyes. "Your mother and I…"

Zack looked at his plate; he felt he might start crying, too, just like his father. "I just thought maybe," Zack said, "if we went to the fair…"

"She's not coming back," his father said. "She's not ever coming back."

"Dad!" Ruth said. "Do you need to say it like that?"

Their father stood abruptly, dropping his arm from his face. "It's been so hard on all of us," he said weakly. "All of us." He looked as though he was going to explain something more, but instead he exhaled heavily and said, "I'm sorry."

Zack's mother suddenly moved both hands to her face as she remained seated.

There was a tense, heavy silence around the table. Ethan looked up and turned to Zack, who continued staring at his plate, but the girls were looking at their father to see what he might say next.

Without any warning, Zack bolted from his chair, dashed into the hallway, and raced up the stairs to his room, where he slammed his door and threw himself onto his bed. He put his face into his pillow and pictured his sister the last time he'd seen her, darting through the people on the sidewalk; and then, as always, he thought about what he might have done to keep her from rushing away. He lay like that for a long while; and when, finally, he heard his siblings and his mother departing for their outing to town, he couldn't figure out if he felt sad or relieved. When he was sure the others were gone and only his father remained, working in one of the rooms below, he sat up on his bed and began watching through his window for any sign of Ann.

Just before three o'clock—and after making his way through several chapters of the third Falcons and Bandits book, *Johnny Swan*—Zack decided to go outside.

His father was working on the window casing in one of the bedrooms on the first floor. Zack hurriedly announced he was going out and would be back shortly, and then he began to turn to leave; but his father put his hammer down loudly and looked at Zack without answering. The two of them stood in place, staring awkwardly at each other for a moment.

"I'm sorry for what I said at lunch, Zack," his father said. "And for the way I said it."

Zack looked at the floor and tried to push the memory from a few hours before—of his father looking sad and angry and confused all at once—from his mind.

"It's all right," he said. A moment's silence followed. "I'm just gonna go for a walk."

"Sounds good. Don't go far, okay?" When Zack didn't respond, his father said, as cheerily as he could, "You, outdoor-goer person," and left it at that as he returned to his work.

Zack moved off down the hallway and departed through the rear door. He stood for a moment gazing at the Tower across the field; but although he'd left the house with every intention of walking toward it—maybe even visiting the cave—he decided to head into the woods, along the trail he and his brother and sisters had taken to the swimming holes. Just as he entered the shade of the forest, he saw a blue T-shirt flitting through the trees ahead and realized Ann was skipping toward him along the trail.

"Zack!" she called as she looked up. "I was coming to see you."

"Hey, Ann," he said, and he took off jogging toward her. "Wow, I'm glad you were coming this way. If you'd gone to the Tower, I would have missed you."

They stopped before each other.

"I haven't seen you in days," Zack said.

"I know. My mom wasn't feeling well, and then she was also

working a lot, so I was always home or at the restaurant." She pointed ahead. "I was thinking of going to your house."

Zack was so surprised to hear this that he gave a small laugh without meaning to. "If my brother and sisters were there, that would have been great. But they're gone." He looked behind him, through the trees and toward his house.

"Then why don't we go hiking together?" she said. "I can show you a place you'll really like."

"Lead the way," Zack said.

They passed a pleasant twenty minutes winding through the trees, Ann pausing at each fork in the trail to consider and then point out the direction they needed to head. Zack told her all about the fireworks show and how he'd left her a note at the cave and how he and his family were making great progress on fixing up the house. Ann explained that she'd had to sit in her mother's restaurant for several days on end because there'd been so many customers, and it had been almost impossible for her to get away long enough to come over to this side of the forest.

"I kept wanting to leave you a note or something," Ann said. "Like we promised."

"At least you're here now," Zack said. The trail was narrow, hemmed in by vine maples; tall fir trees loomed above, and the entire forest around them was shaded and cool. Something about the slant of afternoon light through the trees made Zack think of the strange cabin he and his siblings had found.

"Hey," he said, "have you ever seen this old cabin that's kind of near a couple of nice swimming holes? It's really run-down."

"Those two swimming holes?" Ann said. "One's higher than the other, on top of a little waterfall. Is that the place you mean?"

"Yeah, that's it exactly. We all went swimming there a few days ago, and we found this cabin in the woods right nearby."

"That belonged to Orland Wetherill," Ann said matter-of-factly. "It wasn't his cabin where he lived, but it's where he liked to write and work. At least, that's what my father used to tell me."

"Who's Orland Wetherill?"

Ann stopped and looked at Zack as if he'd asked what state they lived in. "He's the guy who made the stone building. The Tower."

"He made it?" Zack said as Ann resumed walking. It startled him to think that the Tower had actually been built by a real person—for some reason, he'd never thought much about its beginnings. It had been a place that people visited, it had become neglected, and now it sat silently just beyond his family's property; Zack was intrigued to think that there had been a time when it didn't exist and that a person—Orland Wetherill, apparently—had made it.

"He didn't make it himself," Ann said. "He was more like the person who sort of thought it up. I don't know what you call them. He made it up or drew it or something."

"An architect!" Zack said. "That's what my dad does. Or, he did before we moved out here."

"Yes, Orland Wetherill was the architect. He lived here a long time ago, and my father said that he used to go to that cabin you're talking about so he could do his work. It was quiet, I guess, and he liked that."

"You know a lot about the history here."

Ann shrugged. "I've lived here my whole life." She stopped abruptly and looked to Zack with a tiny smile, as though she was about to surprise him with something she was certain he would like.

"We're just about there," she said quietly. "This is one of my favorite places to go."

She motioned him onward with a hand and continued walking, both of them in silence now. The trail curved left and then right; and then, as it passed between two massive cedars, it seemed to come to an end. Ann halted, and a peculiar feeling came over Zack, as if the hush of the forest had deepened. Cedars stood all around them, Zack saw, like delicate brown columns positioned in a deliberate arrangement, a ring that embraced Ann and him. He looked up and saw that the two trees they'd passed were part of ten or so that formed a circle, and that he and Ann stood at the center of it, surrounded by an enfolding perimeter of majestic and tall trees. The feeling was thrilling and strange, something like what Zack sometimes felt on those occasions when his parents took the family to temple for Shabbat services, and everything felt solemn and peaceful—and safe.

"Wow," Zack said, continuing to gaze upward, the light filtering through the cross-hatching of limbs that rose high above, a canopy of green and brown. "This is incredible."

"I know," Ann said. "I love this place."

Zack looked to her and then at the trees around them. "How did they all grow in a circle like this?"

Ann shrugged. "I don't know. My father used to say someone must have planted them like this a long time ago."

"That's for sure," Zack said, looking up again. The trees seemed to be at least one hundred feet tall, maybe more, and the circle was about one-third of that across. "This has been here for ages."

With a deliberate motion, Ann put a finger to her lips. "Hardly anyone knows about this place," she said.

Zack took her meaning and held a hand out to her. "Secret," he said, with a note of finality in his voice. "Another deal!"

Ann shook his hand and laughed. "That's right!" she said, before approaching one of the trees and running her fingers across its strip-like bark.

"Hey, Zack," she said, "do you want to be an architect like your dad?"

"Sometimes I think I want to be a doctor, but I'm not sure."

"A doctor! That would be great. Helping people who get sick, and all that."

"My sister says you have to go to school forever, so I don't know. But that's kind of what I think about sometimes. What about you?"

"I want to write poems. I really love doing that, and I do it all the time. You want to hear one? It's kind of a funny one, and I just made it up a few days ago." Without waiting for Zack to answer, Ann stood up straight beside the tree, removed her hand from the bark, and began to recite from memory:

I love to live in Vista Point
My finger has a double joint
Sometimes it makes a sound like crack
I met a boy whose name is Zack

"What do you think?" she said.

It took Zack a moment to realize she was done, but once the rhythm of the lines had finished spinning in his head, he gave her a thumbs-up.

"I like it," he said. "It was funny. You should keep making poems."

"I'm going to. I'm going to keep making them, and that's what I'm going to be. A poem maker."

"A poet." Zack felt in his pocket for his arrowhead and ran his fingers over it.

"That's right." She pointed over Zack's shoulder. "That cabin is really close, if you know the trail. I'll show you."

A few minutes later, the two of them stood in front of Orland Wetherill's cabin, exactly as Zack and his siblings had done several days before. It looked just as desolate as it had then, forgotten, the moss on its roof a bright green and very thick.

"I wonder when he stopped coming here," Zack said after Ann mentioned that her mother's restaurant had some pictures of Orland Wetherill on its walls. "It looks like it's been abandoned for years."

"I haven't been here in a while," Ann said, studying the broken window before them. She seemed distracted—or puzzled, Zack thought, as though she'd noticed something she hadn't expected.

Ann moved to the door and seemed to be examining the top of the sill. Zack had a feeling she might reach for the rusty door handle.

"My brother said we shouldn't go in."

"Look at that," Ann said, pointing to a spot just above the door. "There's something there."

Zack came and stood beside her to look at what she was pointing to. Affixed to the space above the sill but just below the eave was a plaque—something thin and metallic, though it was so dulled with grime and age that it was almost indistinguishable from the wood of the cabin.

"There's something written on that," Zack said.

"The color was a little different from the wood," Ann said. "That's why I saw it."

Zack turned to see a fallen alder on the ground a few feet behind them, broken into several lengths. "Hey, let's roll that one part of the tree over here, and I can stand on it. Maybe I can see what that thing says."

A moment later, after some maneuvering of the log and a careful positioning of it beside the door, Zack was standing on it and was just able to reach a hand to the plaque. Carefully, steadying himself with one hand and with Ann pressing on his lower back to hold him in place, Zack wiped at the metal with his fingers. The dirt flaked away slowly, and an embossed series of letters emerged. Zack hopped onto the ground, and he and Ann looked at the plaque.

"*The ninth is one*," Zack read. He turned to Ann and squinted. "The ninth is one?"

"What does that mean?" Ann said, but Zack just shrugged in answer. She stared at the plaque and pressed her face forward, as though hoping to make out something on it the two of them might have overlooked.

"Maybe there's something missing," she said. "Like it's supposed to keep going."

"*The ninth is one of something*?" Zack said. "Like that?"

"Yeah," Ann said. "Because it doesn't make sense the way it is."

"I agree." He paused. "But did you notice something? 'One of nine'? Like on the medallion in the Tower?"

"Kind of the same!" Ann said.

"Orland Wetherill must have put that message on the medallion. There's something to do with the number nine." Zack looked at the plaque again. "I wish we knew what it meant."

"Me too," Ann said. She glanced at the window of the cabin again, and Zack felt once more that she was distracted by something.

"You okay?" he said.

"It just looks so old," Ann said. "Older than I remember it." She sighed. "I'm just glad we found that message there. Maybe it can help us figure out what the medallion means."

"I hope so." He waited for Ann to say something, but she kept looking at the plaque. "You sure you're okay?"

Ann put a hand to her belly. "Just getting hungry is all."

"You want to come to my house for a snack?"

She narrowed her eyes, appeared to be giving the idea some consideration. "I'd better go home," she said finally, and then she pointed to a trail that forked off to the east. "I can take this one. It's quickest."

"Okay," Zack said, glancing at the clearing far behind them where the swimming hole was. It was odd to him, how she'd decided so suddenly that she needed to head home. "I know how to get to my house from here."

"I'll try to come to the cave again soon, okay?" Ann said. "I'll leave you a note. Or I'll wait by the Tower and maybe you'll see me." With a glance at the plaque, she said, "*The ninth is one*. I'll ask my mother about it. Maybe she knows something." She continued staring at the plaque. "I wish I could see my dad again. He knew everything about Vista Point."

They both remained silent for a moment, and then Zack said, "I'd better get home, too. But I'll see you soon, okay?"

"Okay," Ann said, and after she turned to follow the trail away from the cabin, Zack watched her disappear into the woods.

Something flitted through the trees, and Zack turned to see a bird—a Steller's jay once again—landing on a branch above the cabin and looking at him.

"You must live here," Zack said to the bird, which sat bobbing its head left and right and then cawed at him once.

Zack sighed. "Okay, I'm going," he said, turning to the swimming hole and the trail home.

Is it all true, what Ann says? Zack thought as he walked. He felt certain there was more to what she'd said than she'd revealed. He enjoyed being with her and was glad to have become friends with her, but some of the things she'd told him seemed not to make sense.

As he made his way down the side of the waterfall and toward the lower pool, he heard the jay give out one last caw.

— *Eleven* —

REVELATION OF A
SECRET

I t became apparent to the kids that the visit from Horatio Cuvallo had rattled their mother and father. Both of them were anxious and distracted for the next couple of days. Something the man had said had flustered both of them more than they were letting on. Their father drove to the county office in Thornton Falls on the very day Horatio appeared, and he was gone for several hours. Their mother holed up in the den that same day and began reviewing some of her files and online documents; she seemed irritable whenever one of the kids spoke to her.

"That man was a total crank," their father muttered on several occasions—over dinner on the day Horatio had appeared, while cooking omelets the morning of the Fourth of July, while driving to see the fireworks—but even his dismissiveness struck the kids as an indication that he was uneasy. "Not even worth discussing," he would add. Neither he nor their mother had much of anything to say about it.

"They found out *something*," Ruth said as she and the three others hiked through the woods on Saturday morning, the day after Zack had gone to Orland Wetherill's cabin with Ann. They were heading for "the pools," as they now called the swimming holes they'd discovered.

"They just don't want to tell us what it is," Ethan said.

"I'm positive Mom and Dad made sure everything was okay before they bought the house," Miriam said. "It's not like they're not smart. *Einsteins*? Remember? Like, *geniuses*?"

Each of the kids had been teased about their last name so many times over the years that it had become a family joke, one they used often with one another. None of them minded it, really, when other kids at school made fun of their name—there were plenty of last names that might sound funny or bring undesirable associations to mind. To have people tease you for being *smart*, though, seemed like a positive thing to the kids, even though none of them had much aptitude for math. Their father had a little joke where he often mixed up the words *relativity* and *relatively* ("When it came to baseball," he would say, "my fastball was relativity fast compared with the other guys in Little League"). Their mother also referred to him as "Albert" every once in a while, which only caused their father to muss up his hair and gaze upward as if studying the heavens.

"But what if it turns out we really can't run a bed-and-breakfast out here?" Ruth said. "How will Mom and Dad make a living?" She stopped in place and lifted her arms at each side in a display of shock. "What if we go bankrupt or something? *The Einsteins were, for a time, one of the more well-off families in Vista Point, until...*"

"You've got to be kidding," Miriam said, trudging onward. "Let's get to the swimming hole!"

"Hottest day of the year so far," Ethan said to Zack, as if to make clear he wanted to ignore the girls' conversation. "I've been tracking it in my notebook."

"*It was a good thing the summer was so warm, because the newly homeless Einstein family hadn't yet bought good sleeping bags,*" Ruth began.

"Ahhh!" Miriam yelled, and she dashed off ahead of the others, who quickly followed.

An hour later, the four kids were sitting on the grass beside the larger swimming hole—"the big pool," the kids called it—Zack had discovered atop the ledge, drying off in a patch of sunlight and taking in the warmth of the day. Bits of cottonwood fluff drifted through the beams of light; the water that fed the pool trickled gently. Zack enjoyed lying on his back with his eyes closed beside the water and feeling the air and the sun on his skin. When he concentrated very hard and the others became silent, he felt as though he had been lying alone next to the water for ages, as though he'd fallen asleep a long time ago and no one had disturbed him or made him leave.

"I'm glad you're coming out more with us, Z," Ethan said, and Zack opened his eyes and squinted into the sky. He'd fallen asleep.

"Me too," Ruth said.

"Me three," added Miriam. "Seriously, it's the best when it's all four of us together. Besides, you found this place, Zack."

Zack sat up slowly and stretched. He had been spending more time with his siblings lately—there was no doubt about it—and as they sat together now relaxing in the sun, he had a strong desire to tell them about what he'd seen at the cabin, though he couldn't figure out how to explain it without mentioning Ann. Miriam was dead set against returning to the cabin, too, so there was no way to somehow have all of them "happen" upon the plaque over the door. He'd wanted to ask about Orland Wetherill at the dinner table the night before by way of learning more—but he decided to wait to bring up the topic. He didn't want to answer any questions that might arise over his interest in the man who'd designed the Tower.

"Do you think we'll see those lights again?" Zack said. "Across the river?"

There had been no repeat of the flashing lights, at least on those evenings after dark when the four kids had sat watching in front of the Tower. Their interest in pursuing the mystery had faded, and they'd only gone to investigate a handful of times after those first few days; but the incident had remained an unsolvable and vexing puzzle to all of them.

"What makes you ask that?" Miriam said.

"I'm just wondering," Zack said.

"I've been studying up on Morse code," Ethan said. "We used it a little at Scout camp." Ethan had brought a notebook and pen with him on those times when the kids had waited by the Tower, all in hope of jotting down the sequence of flashes should they recur; but so far there had been nothing to record.

"Mom was probably right," Ruth said. "It was just someone goofing around that one night."

"Speaking of the Tower," Miriam said, "let me show you guys something."

She pulled her small backpack to her, reached inside, and drew out a piece of paper that she unfolded and held up to show the others. Zack looked—it appeared to be a printout of something from a website.

"I was thinking how we were talking about fixing up the Tower someday, so I did a little research at the library." Miriam wiggled the page. "I printed this out—the history of the Tower."

The three others sat up and drew close together. Zack was riveted all of a sudden, couldn't wait to hear what his sister would reveal. Miriam examined the paper and began to read:

"The original idea for a rest stop at Vista Point came from Or-land Wetherill, the consulting engineer for the Grand River Highway and an architect renowned for his work in stone and glass. Wetherill proposed 'an observatory from which the view both up and down the Grand could be contemplated in silent communion with the infinite.'"

"Read that last part again," Ruth said as Miriam looked up. "The 'silent communion' part." And once Miriam had repeated herself, Ruth simply shook her head languidly—as if she'd just heard a beautiful piece of music—and said, "That sounds incredible." She looked to Ethan. "We really should find a way to convince Mom and Dad to buy the Tower and open it up."

"Listen to this, though," Miriam said. "There's more. About the inside."

As she started to read, a pang of guilt ran through Zack: He'd been inside the Tower and knew how magnificent it was, but his brother and sisters could only wonder about it. Still, he was fascinated to learn more about Orland Wetherill and his design for the Tower.

"Stairs lead from the rotunda to an elevated viewing platform at the base of the dome," Miriam read. *"The exterior is gray sandstone with a green tile roof, and the interior is extensively finished in marble. The dome interior has golden-bronze lining. The upper windows feature opalescent glass, with similar colored glass at the tops of the windows at the main level."*

She looked up. "This is all from the original description, back when they built it in 1895."

"Keep reading," Ethan said.

"The floors and stairs in the rotunda are Tokeen Alaskan marble. Most of the interior of the rotunda is light cream and pink Kasota limestone, including the hand-carved drinking fountains. The roof is surfaced with matte-glazed green tiles."

Miriam looked up. "I don't understand a lot of the descriptive stuff," she said.

"Keep reading!" Ruth insisted. "Is there more?"

"A little bit," Miriam said. "About the carvings inside." She resumed reading. *"Nine faces of Native Americans and local pioneers are atop the columns in the rotunda. Their identities are unknown. Between these columns are carved stone memorials depicting native plants."*

Miriam glanced up with a glint in her eyes. "And listen to this. This is the coolest part of all." She returned to the page. *"A silver medallion is set at the center of the rotunda's ceiling, with the words 'One of Nine' inscribed on it and rimmed with three lines of letters in apparently random order in concentric circles. The mystery of this medallion has never been publicly divulged, and there is no indication of who—Wetherill or some other of the original planners—placed it or for what purpose. 'I would ask that anyone who solves the message keep the answer to themselves,' Wetherill once said. 'Allow each person to discover the answer on their own.'"*

Miriam set the paper down with finality. "A silver medallion! With a mystery to it!"

"Is there a picture of the medallion?" Ethan said.

"No pictures," Miriam said, holding up the page. "Just that description."

"I wish we could see what's written on the thing," Ethan said. "I'd love to figure it out."

"The inside of the Tower sounds too incredible for words," Ruth said.

"For you, that's saying a lot," Miriam said.

"And a secret message?" Ruth said. "Come on! We gotta look into this!"

"For sure," Miriam said, sitting up tall. "I'm dying to look inside."

"I've been in it," Zack said quietly. The words came out of him before he even knew he would speak them—though as he did, he realized he'd been wanting to tell his siblings the truth from the moment he'd first entered the stone building.

"What?" Ethan said. "The Tower?"

Miriam shifted her eyes to Ruth and then to Ethan, quickly, before fixing them on Zack. "You've been inside, Z? When?"

The glade had gone silent once more, in that way Zack had become accustomed to—the mood had shifted instantly, and Zack saw on the faces of his brother and sisters not the delight and surprise he'd been hoping for but something else, something he hadn't expected: They weren't sure if they could believe him.

"A few days after we got here," Zack said. "That first time all of you went to Thornton Falls with Mom. I was outside, and I went to the Tower. I don't know why, but I tried the doors and they were open."

"And you went in?" Ruth said. "For real?"

"Yes," Zack said a bit too insistently. "You won't tell on me, will you? I know I wasn't supposed to do it."

Ruth turned to Ethan. "Aren't the doors locked?"

Ethan tightened his lips and began to scratch his jaw. "We've never actually tried to open the doors," he said. "At least, I haven't. And I don't even think Mom and Dad have tried." He looked at Zack. "They asked us not to go in there."

Zack looked to Miriam and then Ruth and then Ethan, each of whom was gazing at him. "Maybe the historical society people forgot to lock it, I don't know. But when I went in there, it was just like the stuff Miriam read. Even the medallion. And it's really nice. Like, not run-down or anything, aside from the broken windows." Zack was intent now on proving the genuineness of his story, though he resolved not to mention anything about Ann or about the second time he'd been in the Tower. It seemed enough to let his siblings know he'd disobeyed their parents on one occasion.

"Zack," Miriam said softly, a note of question in her voice, but Zack didn't give her a chance to continue.

"I know what you're gonna say," he said. "You're going to ask if I'm lying about it or making it up. But I'm not." He looked from face to face, and no one spoke. The familiar and discomfiting sensation of solitude—of being with the others but not being understood—flooded Zack.

"Just look at this," he said finally. He reached for his backpack, unzipped the small top pocket, and withdrew a piece of paper that he unfolded and presented to Ethan, who glanced at it and allowed his face to go blank.

"What's on there?" Ruth said.

Ethan glanced up and extended the paper to her just as Miriam scooted beside her.

"*One of nine*," Ethan said, reciting what he'd just read. "And the other lines, too. They're all on there." He looked to Zack. "You really *have* been inside, haven't you?"

Zack merely sat in silence, looking off toward the trees beyond which stood Orland Wetherill's cabin, the place he'd visited with Ann. He couldn't figure out if he was betraying her friendship by sharing everything with his brother and sisters, or if he was helping to make it easier for Ann and him—for everyone—to visit the Tower if they chose.

Miriam looked up from the paper. "We need to see inside the Tower ourselves, if we can," she said. "Zack, you shouldn't have gone in there, but it's already done. We should check it out for sure, though."

"Not without Mom and Dad," Ethan said. "We should all go together."

"What if the doors are locked?" Ruth said. "I mean, it must

have been a mistake that they were open when Zack went in. They must be locked now."

"Maybe Mom and Dad can get the key from the historical society," Ethan said.

"I like that plan," Ruth said.

"That's fine," Miriam said.

"You guys aren't going to tell, are you?" Zack said. "I know it was wrong. I just don't want to get in trouble."

"I suppose we can keep it to ourselves," Ethan said. "But you have to promise us you won't go there again without us."

"Promise us?" Miriam said.

"I promise," Zack said. "Next time it will be all of us together."

— *Twelve* —

THE CAMP IN THE FOREST

After the kids discussed the Tower some more and then continued splashing around in the water for a bit, they gathered their towels and backpacks and left the swimming hole. When they reached a fork in the trail just north of the spot and were about to head west to return home, Ethan stopped and looked to the eastern portion of the trail and pointed to it.

"We haven't gone this way before," he said. "You guys want to take a little detour?"

"Lead the way, Mr. Eagle Scout," Miriam said, and the kids veered eastward and began trekking through the woods.

The trees were higher and thicker here, with dense stands of cedar that stood tall enough in places that the air held a brisk coolness; the sunlight was muted deeply, bathing everything in a dim emerald light. For moments at a time, as Zack walked behind his brother and sisters, he closed his eyes and absorbed all of it. There was something, too, about the atmosphere of the forest here that caused the kids to speak quietly, in hushed tones—when they spoke at all.

The four Einsteins walked in silence for several long minutes, and then Miriam stopped abruptly and lifted a hand to signal the others to stop, too.

"Do you hear something?" she whispered, cocking her head to one side and listening.

Zack looked ahead on the trail and listened. The sound of music came to him from far off, a slow melody of notes he recognized as a voice.

"Someone's singing," he said.

"Yeah," Ethan said. "I hear it, too. It sounds like a woman."

Ruth pointed ahead. "Let's keep going. See who it is."

Ethan strode forward, and the others followed, though everyone moved more deliberately now, placed their steps carefully, cautiously, not wanting to make too much noise. They advanced on the trail, and the singing—a tune that Zack had never heard before but that sounded somehow familiar, like a lullaby, maybe—grew louder, though the song was unhurried and sounded sad.

"What is she singing?" Miriam whispered. "It sounds like another language."

"*Lima anak* something something?" Ruth said in perplexity. "Is that Spanish?"

"Doesn't sound like it," Miriam said.

"Shhh!" Ethan said.

The trail climbed a steep but short incline; and when the four kids reached the top, a spread of open forest lay before them that, though clear of trees, was brimming with life and activity. Four large log cabins—their walls lacquered honey-brown, and each with smoke coming from its chimney—stood at the corners of the broad expanse; an enormous garden, surrounded by a split-rail fence, lay off to a side. A pen with several goats in it sat beside one of the houses; small sheds were scattered here and there, some with rakes and hoes leaning against them; a sturdy treehouse—at least twenty feet above the ground—that looked like a spaceship clung to the trunk of a fir near one of the houses. Lines of drying clothes were strung between trees next to a couple of the houses; a large fire was dancing in a rock-rimmed pit near the garden; and three enormous white banners—at least as big as the oversized American flag Zack had seen flapping on the huge pole during the Fourth of July celebration—were stretched across the branches of a cedar. Of all the sights, Zack found that these banners drew his eye most immediately: On them were intricate patterns painted in delicate black lines with meticulous care.

A few people—including a couple of kids who looked younger than Zack—were on folding chairs or standing around the fire.

One of the people—a blond woman cradling a baby and swaying slowly—was singing as the others listened; but right as her eyes landed on Zack and his siblings, she stopped singing, and all the other people with her turned to look at the Einsteins in silence.

"This is what Mom and Dad were telling us about," Miriam said in an excited whisper, just barely loud enough for Ethan, Ruth, and Zack to hear her. "The people who live out here by themselves!"

Zack's heart was beating quickly, partly because it seemed alarming to have come across so many unknown people out in the woods, but also because he felt certain he was going to see Ann. He studied the faces of the people around the fire. They looked to Zack like a group of people on a camping trip, like the families or groups he and his family had seen when they'd packed their tents and gear in their car and spent the weekend at the ocean or by some mountain lake. It made him wonder what he'd expected the people in the forest to look like. He scanned the area a couple of times.

"Hi," one of the men beside the fire said. He wore jeans and a blue T-shirt; he looked to Zack pretty much like the men who had worked with his father at the Valencia & Hartnett Firm.

"Hello?" Ethan said tentatively, raising a hand.

"Can we help you?" the man said. Two of the other men stood.

"Maybe we should leave them alone," Miriam said, again in her quietest whisper; Zack was just a couple of feet from her, but it was almost impossible even for him to hear her.

"We were just hiking," Ruth answered the man. "But we're about to head back the other way." She made a dramatic swoop of her arm to indicate that the four of them were set to reverse their tracks.

"Hiking?" a different man said. He had black hair and was wearing shorts that had been cut off from a pair of jeans. He took a few steps toward the kids. "Do you live around here?"

"Yeah," Ethan said. "Not too far."

"Ethan," Miriam whispered again, her tone imploring and—Zack thought—scared. "Let's go."

"Well, you're welcome to join us for a few, if you like," the first man said.

Two women appeared from behind a cabin on the far side of the fire, and then two children—maybe five years old, both—raced out of another cabin. There were close to twenty people now regarding the Einsteins in a way Zack couldn't figure out: He wasn't sure if they were uncomfortable because they'd been discovered or if they were displeased at the encroachment—or if they were just curious.

"We should probably get back home," Miriam said. "We're sorry we disturbed you." She reached for Ruth's shirt and gave a small tug.

"No disturbance," the black-haired man said. He spread both arms wide and looked all around. "The forest belongs to everyone."

"Well, we sure appreciate the offer," Ethan said. "But we'll get going."

The black-haired man turned to the others around the fire, and someone said something to him Zack couldn't quite hear. The man looked back at the kids and said, "Are you the ones who moved into the old Vale place?"

"Don't tell them," Miriam whispered.

"Stop that, Mir," Ruth whispered back, and then she looked at the black-haired man and said, "That's right. We're fixing it up, and we…" She faltered, glanced at Zack as if trying to figure out what to say next. "And we're happy to know you are our neighbors."

The first man said, "Well, so are we," and then he waved to the kids. "You have a good day, okay? We appreciate you being friendly."

"I like the artwork," Zack called, pointing to one of the banners, even as he felt in his pocket for his arrowhead.

"So do we," the blond woman called. "Thank you."

"Hope to see you again," the black-haired man said.

A few of the others around the fire smiled and waved to the kids, and the blond woman resumed her song. The others returned to whatever they'd been doing before—relaxing or contemplating or listening to the woman singing—and turned away. It was as if they had retreated into their own world, and Ethan, Miriam, Ruth, and Zack had disappeared.

Zack surveyed the camp one last time, still hoping to spot Ann; and then he felt Ruth pulling him by his shirt, and he and the other three turned to descend the little path that had brought them to the spot overlooking the clearing. When they reached the bottom of the small hill, Ethan said, "Let's get home!"; and the three others took off racing behind him as if they were being chased. No one said a word—no one even looked back—for several minutes, until they'd put a good long distance between them and the camp.

When they stopped to catch their breath finally, Miriam stared back at the trail in the direction they'd come and said, "Well, that was interesting."

"You were scared!" Ruth said. "Admit it."

"They were nice," Ethan said. "But it was kind of strange to stumble onto their place like that." He looked at Miriam. "You *were* kind of scared, Mir."

"No, I wasn't," she said. "It's just, I don't think we should go around telling people in the middle of nowhere who we are and where we live."

"It's different out here," Ruth said. "Not like the city. Those people were super nice, and I think it was fine to talk to them. They already knew who we were." She looked at Zack. "And I agree with you, Z. That artwork of theirs was cool."

"The whole place was cool," Zack said, still disappointed that he hadn't seen Ann. "It was…," he began. A thought came to him, something he hadn't considered at all when the camp had been right before him but that felt imperative now.

"You okay, Zack?" Ethan said.

"Susan would have liked seeing it," Zack said.

Miriam's face arranged itself instantly into something that looked like frustration. She took two steps toward Zack and pointed to him.

"Do you always have to do that?" she said.

"Mir," Ruth said softly. "Stop."

"No," Miriam said. "I'm not mad or anything—just…this

116

always happens." She looked to Zack once again. "Whenever we're doing anything, it's like you can't stop trying to take us back to Susan. She got hit by a car. She had a funeral. It's the worst, and I hate it, and I miss her just like you do, and I think about her all the time. But we can't just keep bringing her up forever no matter what happens."

"Stop, Miriam," Ethan said. "You're the one going on about her now. Everyone else is fine."

"Everyone?" Miriam said, pointing to Zack. "We see a bunch of people in the woods, and Zack starts talking about Susan, and everyone is fine?"

A silence descended on the four kids, as deep as any that had held while they'd watched the people in the woods. Zack looked from Miriam to Ruth to Ethan and then back to Miriam. He had no idea what he felt or what he wanted to say, and so the words that came out of him surprised him just as much as they surprised the others.

"You just want to forget her!" he shouted.

"No, she doesn't, Zack," Ruth said.

But Zack was in no mood to listen. He looked at Ruth and then at Miriam, and he felt something inside of him welling up so strongly, he was afraid he would start to cry.

"All of you do!" he yelled, and then he turned and ran as quickly as he could, leaving the others behind, hoping he would outrun them. All he wanted was to reach the cave, hide himself within it, and be alone.

— *Thirteen* —

DINNER WITH THE BIGELOWS

Later that afternoon, once Zack had tired of pouting in the cave—and after leaving a note for Ann indicating he would try to meet her there on the coming Monday—he trudged home to find that his parents were half-worried and half-angry with him and that his brother and sisters were content to give him his space. Dinners were mandatory, though, and so Zack had not been allowed to remain in his room; but he ate quickly and perfunctorily (saying nothing when the others explained to their parents that they'd seen the people who lived in the woods and that the encounter had been uneventful) and left as quickly as he could to resume reading *Snowy Holiday*, the fourth Falcons and Bandits book, alone in his room before falling asleep. The next day, Sunday, was spent in similar solitary fashion. At four in the afternoon, his mother knocked on his door and explained he needed to be ready to depart at six o'clock.

"We've been invited to our new neighbors' home for dinner," she said. "The Bigelows. The nice couple down the road."

Zack said nothing.

"And we're all going," his mother added, "and we're all going to have a great time."

As it turned out, his mother was more than correct.

Rydell and Juanita Bigelow lived a quarter mile west of the Einsteins, along the main road; and on the evening after the day when the four kids had stumbled onto the camp in the woods, all six of the Einsteins found themselves comfortably seated at the Bigelows' dining room table in the elderly couple's cozy cabin. Decorative quilts—of farm scenes, winter mountains, graceful patterns, fields of wildflowers, and much more—hung here and there on the log walls of the room, and display cabinets and hutches filled with ceramic figurines and old books stood in every corner. Zack, who'd not said a word on the walk to the Bigelows' home, gaped in wonder when the Einsteins entered the house right up until dinner was served.

"I'm very biased in what I'm about to mention," Rydell announced after saying grace but before anyone had touched their food, "but this fried chicken you're about to eat is unmatched not only in this county but in this entire half of the state. Maybe the entire state itself."

He spoke with so much casual conviction—as if relating the weather forecast—that Zack believed him instantly. Besides,

Rydell Bigelow had kind eyes and a pleasantly broad face, he wore wool pants and suspenders, and he bore enough of a resemblance to Grandpa Howard on his father's side that Zack was put at ease from the moment he stepped in the door. What's more, Juanita, in her clunky glasses and with her white hair pulled back into a single braid, laughed so sweetly at just about every other thing Rydell said, it was enough to make Zack nearly put aside all the anger he'd been nurturing for the past day and a half.

As Zack and the other Einsteins sat at the Bigelows' table and enjoyed the meal ("With a veggie option for the young lady!" Juanita had announced as she brought a hot pasta dish out for Ruth), all the bad feelings drifted away from Zack. The couple's cabin was very small—especially when compared to the Einsteins' place—and their property was very modest (a garden, three apple trees, and some stone "sculptures" Rydell had piled up years before), but the spirit in the log cabin was too heartening to be held off. Zack felt good once again.

"You like that chicken, don't you?" Rydell asked him at one point, with a wink.

"I do, sir," Zack said. "Thank you."

"I think we all do," Zack's father said. "I'm thinking there could be a Bigelows' Roadside Diner up here one of these days. The place would be mobbed."

Juanita began to laugh, and Rydell sat back and put a hand to one of his suspenders.

"You're the ones we're excited about," Rydell said. "With your place opening just down the road. Been a long time since anything has come along to spice things up around here."

"How long have you two lived here, Mr. Bigelow?" Ethan said.

"Well, I'm from Roseburg originally," Rydell said.

"And I'm from down near Pailey Bay," Juanita said. "But we met years ago when we were working at the locks, and we bought this place in sixty-three, so almost forty years."

"You must have seen a lot of changes," Deborah said.

And with that, Rydell and Juanita began detailing some of the history of the area—the logging that had waxed and waned, the construction of the highway beside the river that had increased tourism to all the famous waterfalls, the time a barge had caught fire on the river, an occasion when an escaped convict had ended up cornered in a restaurant near Silver Chute Falls.

"You know," Rydell said, "that house you're in wasn't always the mansion it is today."

"That's what I understand," Deborah said. "I was doing some research on it."

"Used to be a tiny little place," Rydell said.

"But right near the Vista Point C.S.," Juanita said. "Magical to be that close to such a lovely building."

"C.S.?" Miriam said.

"Comfort station," Rydell said. "You'd call it a rest stop today. That building was kind of run-down when we got here, but then the state tried to fix it up a little. New roof, new bathrooms and walkway. Twenty-five years ago, once the big highway went in, most of the traffic ended up down below. Then the owners of your house—it was a mansion by then—were wealthy enough that they created all sorts of legal tangles about automotive access to the spot and the condition of the road. The state gave up at that point, and the place shut down. It's been empty now for about fifteen years."

"Real shame," Juanita said. "Such a lovely building and constructed with so many high hopes. Hard to believe it's abandoned now."

"We had a gentleman come by last week," Morton said. "He told us he used to live in our house, and he was pretty upset about our presence and the fact that we want to open up a bed-and-breakfast."

Juanita lifted her chin. "That would be Horatio," she said.

"That's right," Deborah said. "Horatio Cuvallo."

"He lived there with his family," Rydell said. "They were there when we bought our place. Just him, his wife, and their young daughter."

"Well, he sure was upset with us," Deborah said.

"He's upset with everyone," Juanita said, not unkindly. "I feel sorry for him. We actually hadn't seen him or heard anything about him for years, and then he popped back up just—when?" She looked to Rydell. "Four or five years ago?"

"That's right," Rydell said. "His wife left him back in about sixty-five and took the girl with her. Horatio went to Vietnam, and that was the last anyone heard of him for years. MIA. Missing in action. We all thought he was dead. Which is how he most likely would have ended up if he'd stayed here all those years ago, as bad off as he was after his wife left. Different man after losing his family. Bitter. I'm afraid he took to drinking a bit, as well. Then he lost the house and property. Couldn't make his payments, and the state took the place. I guess joining the army was his only option."

The Einsteins had stopped eating and were intent on the incidents the Bigelows were relating. Juanita glanced about in what looked like slight embarrassment.

"We didn't mean to dredge up ancient history here," she said. "But you can see maybe why the man is the way he is." She tapped her chest. "Heartache. Unhappy emotions."

"That's such a sad story," Ruth said softly. She was staring forlornly at Juanita. "Did he ever see his wife and daughter again?"

Rydell shrugged. "Who knows? He shocked us all by coming back to the Vista Point area. He was living with a relative somewhere nearby, but I'm not sure if that's still the case. You see him around still, and we all try to be friendly with him. But he's set in his ways."

Zack had been listening to Rydell's and Juanita's words raptly. He already knew, given what Horatio had explained while looming in the doorway of the Einsteins' house several days before, that Horatio had been a soldier; but now the details were filling in. It remained an odd coincidence to Zack, the whole thing—Ann's mention of her father being a soldier and Horatio's claim of the very same thing.

"What was his daughter's name?" Zack said, and everyone looked at him with perplexity.

"Felicia, wasn't it?" Rydell said, looking to Juanita.

"That's right," she said. "Felicia. Lord knows what happened to her and her mother. No one's ever seen them again around these parts, as far as I know."

"Lot of interesting history to this place," Morton said. "I bet there's a story around every bend in the road."

"Best one is about the C.S.," Rydell said.

"We've been calling it the Tower," Ethan said. "Just because of how it looks."

"I like that," Juanita said. "The Tower. We all got so used to calling it the C.S., the name kind of stuck, but the Tower sounds so much better."

"More romantic," Ruth said.

"Well, the story about that place," Rydell continued, "is that if it's well maintained, it can be a real asset not only to this area but to, well, the larger area in general." He looked to Juanita. "Am I telling it right?"

"Pretty much," she said. "It's hard to know how seriously to take it, but when we moved in here, there were still some old-timers who remembered Orland Wetherill himself. He was the main designer behind the C.S. Or, rather, the Tower. After he built it—with plenty of his own money, by the way—it was always a struggle to keep the place open. Two wars and plenty of hard times along the way. Orland's dream never quite materialized, as beautiful as the building is."

"Miriam found some information about him," Ethan said.

Miriam lifted both hands and grinned. "I did, I did."

Their father sighed. "Let Mr. and Mrs. Bigelow continue, please."

"Just Rydell and Juanita is fine," Rydell said. "No need for formality. We're neighbors and friends now. And after dessert, I'm going to regale you with some of my clarinet playing. But, Juanita, you were saying?"

"It's just that we were told that Orland used to claim that there was some sort of charm that needed to be spoken—once a year, apparently—right by the building, and that if the place was kept up nicely and this charm was said, the building would not only attract visitors but become sort of known for its hospitality. Its goodness. Kind of spread the feeling to everyone who came to see it."

"That certainly sounds like something we could use more of in these times," Morton said.

"I couldn't agree more," Rydell said. "It's tough to know if Orland Wetherill really said all those things or if people just made them up. But it's a nice thought. Apparently, people around here used to share that story a lot."

"I heard about that, too," Zack said. "That it was a lucky place."

Once again, everyone at the table looked at him.

"You heard about it?" Miriam said. "Where?"

"Just…," Zack began. "I don't know. Around." He went silent immediately, even as he felt everyone's eyes on him. His face flushed.

Juanita clicked her tongue in approval. "Well, I think it will be a very lucky place now that your family is close by it. That's what I think."

"We should buy it and fix it up, Dad," Ruth said. "What if that story is true?"

Her father gave a little laugh, something mildly exasperated. "It's just a story, honey."

Everyone chuckled—aside from Zack.

"But what if it's true?" Zack said. He thought of the letters written on the medallion. "What if there really is a charm, and if someone says it and the Tower is all cleaned up, it would make it so that…I don't know. It would make it so that everything is good again."

"You have a very generous soul, young man," Juanita said, smiling at Zack.

The feeling of tears welling up in his eyes returned to Zack, only this time he didn't feel his familiar sadness but something hopeful and gentle that surprised him.

"Thank you," he said. And then—tentatively, with a glance at his mother and father first—he added, "Juanita."

"Very nice!" the elderly woman said.

"I think it's time for dessert," Rydell said. "I know I'm ready for it."

"My blueberry scones with ice cream," Juanita said, standing.

"Nothing gets a crowd more prepared for some clarinet music than that!" Rydell said, and everyone laughed.

Zack tried to remember just what had made him so angry at his brother and sisters the day before. "I'm sorry," he said, looking to the three of them as their parents rose to help Juanita bring in the dessert. "About what I said yesterday."

Ethan pumped a fist at him encouragingly. "No worries, Z," he said.

"We took a vote on whether or not to kick you out of the family," Miriam said, not even trying to hold back her smile.

"Three to zero in favor of letting you stay," Ruth said, and she wrapped an arm around Zack's shoulders.

It felt good to back away from the anger and sadness he'd been feeling. But the next day, after Zack made a visit to the cave and found a note from Ann that read *I can't come for a few days*, he felt deflated once again. The words dismayed him because they were so indefinite. He'd been looking forward to seeing Ann—he wanted to ask her if she knew anything more about the legend of the Tower, and he wondered if she might be able to show him any other interesting places nearby—and now he didn't know when he would see her again.

— *Fourteen* —

REVELATIONS AND DOUBTS

Work continued on the house without any letup. The interior was coming along nicely, with all the rooms painted and much of the furniture in place, along with plenty of "antiques" Morton and Deborah had located at thrift stores; two of the five guest bedrooms appeared nearly ready for guests, though the dining room and kitchen still needed plenty of work. The outside of the house was beginning to look presentable after decorative shutters were put on all the windows and the gutters were replaced. The workers had even tidied up the big front lawn and the hedges leading to the mansion.

"We won't be able to keep people away at this rate," their father announced over dinner on Monday.

"You, overly optimistic innkeeper," Miriam said. "How to count your chickens before they crack."

Ruth burst out laughing. "Before they *hatch*. Hatch, hatch! Not *crack*. Gosh, Mir."

"No, wait a minute," Miriam said, looking around uncertainly. "Isn't it like you have to wait until the eggs crack open?" She turned to Ethan. "Maybe?"

"It's *hatch*, Miriam," Ethan said. "Definitely *hatch*." He turned away with a mischievous look on his face. "Maybe someone should *crack* open a book more often."

"When I'm a professional basketball player someday—" Miriam began.

"As we were saying," their mother interrupted, "the house is coming along very nicely, and your father and I appreciate how everyone has pitched in." She gave a pointed, if loving—and slightly humorous—look at Ethan and Miriam in turn. "With their unique talents."

"*Mrs. Einstein often found it necessary to punish her two oldest children for their disobedience,*" Ruth said, and at that point, everyone around the table broke into a good laugh.

The kids had decided not to discuss the Tower with their parents just yet. As upbeat as their mother and father had remained generally, it was clear the visit from Horatio Cuvallo had been deeply unsettling and had initiated some genuine legal investigation on their part. There was nothing definite the kids could point to, but there was something a bit off with their parents whenever the topic of the opening date for the bed-and-breakfast arose. Previously, everything had seemed fixed for a Labor Day start—which, now that the second week of July had arrived, felt closer than ever. Now, though, on those occasions when the subject arose, their parents were vague and evasive. They didn't want to mention Horatio's name, either, nor bring him up in any way. After the dinner with the Bigelows, when Ruth reflected on Horatio's unhappy history at breakfast the next morning, their father dismissed the subject with a brusque, "Most people are about as miserable—or happy—as they make up their mind to be. At least, that's what Abraham Lincoln had to say on the subject."

Following the conversation at the Bigelows', Zack had become even more fascinated by the medallion and the inscription, and he found himself often in his room studying his piece of paper with the words on it or talking to Ethan or the girls about what they might mean.

"It has to be connected to the charm, don't you think?" Miriam said when the four of them began discussing it as they headed out for a morning hike on Thursday.

"I agree," Ethan said. "But, come on, the story the Bigelows told us is just, you know, a story. I mean, someone's supposed to say the charm and then the Tower becomes kind of—what?—magical?"

"Aw, Ethan," Ruth said, "it's more fun to believe it's all true. Don't you think so, Zack?"

"I do," Zack said. "I just wish I could figure out what the words on the medallion mean."

"I think it's one of those codes where there's a key," Ethan said. "And then you substitute the right letters once you know the key to use."

"But almost all the words are nine letters each," Ruth said. "That doesn't seem likely."

"Maybe whoever put it together just grouped them that way," Miriam said.

"I think there's just a bunch of missing letters," Zack said. He'd been giving it a lot of thought and had even read up on codes and secret messages in an old set of encyclopedias his parents had. The one thing he hadn't done was mention to his siblings that he'd seen the plaque over the door at Orland Wetherill's cabin—if he brought that up, it might lead to all sorts of questions about when he'd gone back to the cabin and why. He was convinced, though, that the number nine held the key to solving the medallion's message.

"We have to figure out which letters are missing and then put them in," Zack said.

"I don't know if that sounds right," Miriam said. "I think it's more complicated."

"But what does *One of Nine* mean?" Ruth asked.

The kids had just entered the stand of trees south of their house, across the road, where the ground was more level and the trail wound through several open fields. It was a path they hadn't yet taken. Clouds, low and thin, covered the sky, though it looked as if the sun might break through soon.

"But where did you hear that the Tower was lucky, Zack?" Ethan said. "You said that the other night at the Bigelows'."

"A girl told me," Zack said. He'd been thinking about telling his siblings about Ann for a few days, and he'd decided—when the time felt right—he would reveal only that he'd run into her once in the woods but would not mention anything about the Tower or the cave.

"A girl?" Ethan said, stopping, so that the others stopped, too. "What do you mean?"

"I didn't tell you earlier," Zack said. "But one day when you were all gone, I was playing outside, and a girl came off that trail we take to go to Angel Veil Falls. She said she lives nearby."

Ruth looked to Ethan and then at Zack. "Did you tell Dad?" she said.

"No," Zack said. "Can you not tell him, either? Or Mom? She's just a girl who lives nearby. Her name is Ann."

"Zack," Miriam said, "this is the second thing you've told us now that you don't want Mom and Dad to know about. I don't like this at all."

"But it's not like I broke any rules," Zack said. "I just met a girl who was hiking on the trails."

"How old is she?" Ruth said.

"Susan's age," Zack said.

The awkward silence fell over the four of them once again.

"Zack," Ethan said, "you ran into a girl Susan's age when you were all by yourself one day? And no one else knows about it?"

"I'm not making it up." Zack had prepared himself for this, had expected they would doubt him; and he'd resolved not to feel disappointed by it. "I really saw her. Her name's Ann. She grew up here, and she told me some stuff about the Tower and other things. She said her mom said it was a lucky place. Her mom even works at a restaurant down on the highway." This last fact would be the clincher, he thought, convincing evidence.

"But why would a girl that age just be walking around in the forest?" Miriam said. She turned to Ethan. "Doesn't make sense."

"It's not so bizarre," Ethan said. "I guess. Z, that's all she said about the place? That it was lucky?"

"Yeah. Pretty much."

"And you haven't seen her since?" Ethan said.

Zack didn't want to lie to his brother and sisters—it was more that he just didn't want to tell them everything.

"No, I haven't seen her since," he said.

"Still, it's weird for a kid to be all alone and walking around on the trails like that," Miriam said.

"Did she say where she lives, Zack?" Ruth asked.

"She said she lives on the other side of the forest." Zack realized Ruth had hit upon the very thing that had been bothering him. "But I don't know where."

"Let's keep walking," Miriam said, and she adjusted her backpack and turned to continue on the trail.

"You don't believe me," Zack said—a statement, not a question—as Miriam strode off.

"We should keep going" was all Miriam said, not turning around.

Zack looked at the ground, and for a moment he thought he might say something contrary in return and then race away—again. But he stopped himself, pulled at the straps of his own backpack, and pointed ahead.

"Let's keep going," he said to Ethan and Ruth, neither of whom said a word in return. They simply began walking, and Zack took up the rear.

After twenty more minutes of hiking along this new trail, Ruth halted abruptly and pointed to a clearing up ahead and to the west.

"What's that?" she said, and the others stopped as well and looked in the direction she was facing.

A split-rail wooden fence spanned a clearing within which stood even rows of what looked to Zack like small boulders—until he realized they were tombstones.

"A cemetery," Ethan and Miriam said in unison.

"Let's check it out," Ruth said, and the four kids veered off the trail and onto a narrower, intersecting trail that led to the cemetery, where a wooden gate stood open. They all stopped before it, and no one spoke.

Zack became aware of the same low sound he sometimes sensed at the Tower, an indistinct hum or a faint vibration he could never place. He closed his eyes for a moment, and a thought of Susan came to him instantly, powerfully.

"You first, Eagle Scout," Miriam said to Ethan, and Zack opened his eyes.

Ethan pursed his lips, glanced at his siblings, and then put a hand atop the gate to push it fully open.

"I bet there's a lot of interesting history in this place," he said. "Come on. Let's look around for a few." His gaze fell on his brother. "Okay?"

No one moved. Furtive glances shot from one person to another.

"Is this okay?" Ruth said. "I mean, do you think we should…"

"Let's just take a quick look," Miriam said. She glanced at Zack. "It'll be fine."

Ethan stepped forward in silence, his two sisters behind him. Zack stood in place for a moment and then followed the others.

The four of them fanned out amid the rows, walking slowly as they examined the graves. The cemetery was small, about as wide across as the distance Ethan and Zack put between them when they tossed their miniature football; and it was perfectly flat, with grass that was trim and well maintained. Some of the grave markers were roughly hewn plaques anchored in the ground, though most were upright, and a few were large enough to be imposing.

"Born in 1863!" Miriam exclaimed, pointing at a tombstone before her. "That's during the Civil War."

"This family lost their baby," Ruth said, staring forlornly at a small plaque. "So sad."

"Some people were buried over a hundred years ago," Ethan said, pointing vaguely at the ground all around him. "But some of these are pretty new."

Zack walked along a row of graves, his eyes downcast, trying not to be taken back in his memory to the summer before. And then he stopped as definitely as if someone behind him had placed a hand on his shoulder to bring him to a halt. He lifted his eyes and examined the white marble gravestone before which he stood:

ORLAND WETHERILL

1855–1929

BELOVED SON, HUSBAND, AND FATHER

"ONE OF NINE"

"What do you see, Zack?" Ethan called.

Zack looked up. Ethan, Ruth, and Miriam stood together on the other side of the tombstone and were staring at him; he realized he'd been so lost in his own thoughts he hadn't even noticed them.

"Orland Wetherill," Zack said softly, pointing at the stone. "The man who built the Tower."

The three others approached their brother to take a look for themselves.

"It is!" Ruth said. "And that must be his wife there." She pointed to the tombstone next to Orland's, which indicated a Melrithia Wetherill, who was born in 1861 and passed away in 1945.

"And those must be other members of the family," Miriam said, gesturing to several other markers on either side with the name Wetherill on them. The most recent death was 1967.

Zack was staring at the inscription for Orland Wetherill, though, with no thought to the graves of the others nearby.

"*One of nine*," Ethan said, echoing the words in Zack's head.

"Just like on the medallion," Ruth said quietly.

"That's kind of creepy," Miriam said.

"Why do you think that's written on there?" Zack said without moving his gaze from the words themselves.

"No idea," Ethan said. "But it must have been really important to him."

"It's a clue," Ruth said. "Don't you think? For the words on the medallion."

The humming noise sounded in Zack's head once again, and then his thoughts became clouded by an image of the medallion and something Ann had said to him and thoughts of Susan and the memory of his mother's face that night at the fair and—

"Hey," Ethan said abruptly, and Zack felt his brother clutch his arm. "You okay?"

Zack shook his head as if to rouse himself out of a sleep. "I'm okay," he said unsteadily.

"Well, you look like you're going to faint," Miriam said. "Too much sun or something?"

A cawing sound arose from the forest just beyond the cemetery's fence.

"Look," Ruth said, pointing to a large cedar whose branches extended above a row of graves. "A Steller's jay!" She turned to Miriam and began to laugh. "The same one, Mir, looking for you again!"

Ruth's joke was well intended, but none of the others so much as smiled. They simply peered at the jay, which sat bobbing its head and letting out its harsh cry, a strange and instant agitation. Zack thought back to the cabin and to the plaque he and Ann had found.

"Come on, you guys," Miriam said. "Let's get back on the main trail and have a drink of water." She looked to Zack. "You'll feel better."

Ethan still had a hand on Zack's arm. "You good, Z?"

Zack stared at Orland Wetherill's tombstone once again, quickly, and then at the jay, which continued squawking at them from its branch. "I'm good."

That afternoon, when their mother took Ethan out to practice his driving and the girls were helping their father stain the banister between the second and third floors, Zack slipped off to the cave and found a note from Ann: *I can meet you here tomorrow after lunch.*

— *Fifteen* —

ANOTHER MEETING

Zack spent the next morning reading the first half of *Lark League*, the fifth book in the Falcons and Bandits series; and he remained in his room throughout. He kept wondering how he would be able to get away by himself after lunch, and then his mother and siblings decided they needed to run errands in Thornton Falls, and Zack's dilemma was resolved. By one o'clock, and under the bright mid-July sun, he was crossing the big field north of the house and heading for the woods just east of the Tower. Once there, he looked around to see if Ann might be in sight, maybe angling through the trees; and when he didn't see her, he headed down the slope of the hill, came out of the woods, made his way west across level ground, and then found the stand of cedars and the ancient stump and the cave just beyond. He was expecting it to be deserted, but as he pulled back the overhanging moss and grass, Ann said, "It's you!" and she leaped up to welcome him in.

"You're here," Zack said, stepping inside. "I got your note."

"My mom's been working almost every day," Ann said, sitting back down on the ground almost as quickly as she had arisen. She wore a white T-shirt and blue jeans, just as she had when Zack met her the first time. "So I've been going to the restaurant with her. I haven't come over here for a long time."

Zack sat on the ground opposite Ann; there was plenty of light in the cave, and it was pleasantly cool within.

"I meant to ask you," Zack said. "What is the name of the restaurant, anyway? Where she works?"

"The Double-R Café," Ann said. "She likes it there."

"What do the *R*s stand for?"

Ann shrugged. "I don't know. My mother just works there."

He glanced at the lines carved into the rock at the rear of the cave. Ann turned and looked behind her.

"Those words," she said. "*Ray* and *Jing*."

"Don't you wonder what it means?" Zack said.

"I guess we'll never know."

The two kids caught up for the next several minutes—mostly Zack told Ann about how the house was coming along and how he and his siblings had been spending their days hiking or swimming or helping out where they could. "We keep telling our parents we should fix up the Tower and open it again," he added.

"I'd come every day. I love to look at the river from the stairs. It looks so beautiful from there."

"We went to dinner at our neighbors' house, too. This couple named the Bigelows, who've lived here a long time."

Ann squinted. "What's their name?"

"Bigelow."

"I think I met them before."

"They're really nice. They said there was a charm that has to do with the Tower, and I started thinking maybe all those letters on the medallion had something to do with it. Hey, I forgot! Did you look at all those sentences? The ones we wrote down last time?"

"I started to," Ann said, "and then I gave up. It didn't really make any sense."

The sound of a whistle from far below—some sort of signal from a boat—drifted across the slope outside the cave with a long, sad note.

"If you live on the other side of the woods," Zack said, "why do you like to come all the way over here? I've been meaning to ask you that."

"I love the stone building," Ann said. "The Tower. I love coming to it. Plus, there's the cave here. And I guess mostly it's because my father used to like coming over here to the building, and he would bring me. He used to tell me if I ever got lost, I should go to it and he would find me. He said I wouldn't need to worry, because he would always come for me."

Zack didn't know what to say. He was thinking that if Ann's father had been killed in whatever war he'd been in, there was no way for him to come to her, no way for him to help her if she needed it. But before he could follow this idea all the way through, he stopped himself.

"Sometimes, when we lived in Roseburg, I used to worry about getting lost if I wasn't with my parents or my brother or sisters," Zack said.

"We read a story once in school when I was in first grade," Ann said. "And there was a girl who got lost in the forest, and it took them a long time to find her. I didn't like that story. It was too scary. So my father taught me a system so that he could find me if that ever happened to me. I told him I was scared about getting lost."

Zack felt a shiver go down his spine. "A system? What do you mean?"

"I just mean…," Ann began. "It's kind of hard to explain." She looked at her hands and began scratching a finger.

It was clear to Zack she didn't want to talk about it, but he couldn't figure out why.

"Hey, I meant to tell you," he said, changing the subject. "We saw those people who live in the woods. The ones I told you about."

"Which ones?"

"In the cabins. We ran into them last week."

"I don't know who they are."

"They have a garden and a bunch of goats, and a big firepit. You must have seen them if you've been on all the trails." Zack paused. "It's okay if you know those people. You could tell me."

Ann gave a simple shrug. "But I don't. I've never seen anyone living in the woods like that."

"Well, they were pretty nice to us." Zack went silent, and he realized he was hoping Ann might offer something, divulge something. He was beginning to feel convinced—by Ann's evasiveness and her vague answers—that she lived with the group and was, perhaps, just too embarrassed to share the truth with him for some reason.

"Hey, Ann," Zack said. "You said your father would help you if you got lost, but he was killed in the war, right?"

Ann looked at her hands once again. "I know. But he told me if I ever got in trouble or felt scared, he would help me, so I believe him."

It was impossible for Zack to make sense of what Ann was saying.

"I wish I had brothers and sisters, like you do," Ann said. "That's one of the reasons I like the Falcons and Bandits books so much. All the brothers and sisters are always having adventures together and helping each other out. I think you're lucky."

"We argue sometimes about things," Zack said, "but most of the time they're pretty nice to me." He paused. "Hey, you said the word *lucky* again—like how you once said the Tower was lucky."

Ann reached into the pocket of her jeans and removed the piece of paper on which Zack had written the words from the medallion.

"I was looking at this," she said, "but I couldn't figure anything out. It just seems all jumbled up to me."

"The only thing that makes sense is the *One of Nine* part," Zack said. "I mean, at least those words all go together. And then there was the plaque on the cabin. *The ninth is one.*" He was about to mention something about Orland Wetherill's grave, when Ann began speaking enthusiastically.

"Are you good at multiplication?" she said. "Nines were the hardest for me, but our teacher showed us something that made it fun. She said you take nine times two and it makes eighteen, and then if you add the one and the eight, you end back at nine. And then nine times three is twenty-seven, so if you take the two and the seven together, you still get nine. Do you see what I mean? It works all the way if you keep going."

Zack had never thought about this before, and something in the way Ann explained it made him feel interested to work through more of the possibilities. Before he began, though, he reached for the paper Ann held and studied it for a moment before handing it back to her.

"What are you thinking about?" Ann said.

"*One of Nine,*" Zack said. "*The ninth is one.*"

"Zack!" came a shout from far away.

"Who's that?" Ann said as her eyes went wide.

Zack listened as the cry came again. "That sounds like my sister

Ruth," he said, though this baffled him completely. "But she went with the others about an hour ago."

The call rose once more, this time repeated by Ethan, who added, "Zack, where are you?"

"They sound like they're far away," Ann said.

"Not too far away," Zack said. "I bet they're at the Tower." He stood. "I'd better go."

"Okay. I wish you could stay longer, though."

"Hey, I know! Why don't you come with me? You can meet them."

Ann shook her head quickly. "I'm going to stay here, okay?"

"They're really nice. Seriously. They would like you."

"I'm just going to stay here. Maybe you can come back?"

"I don't know. I'll try, okay?"

Ann stood, smiled, and held out a hand. "Deal!" she said.

Zack shook her hand. "Be careful going back if I don't see you, all right?"

"I'll be okay. Remember what I said about my father?"

It pained Zack to hear those words—he couldn't help thinking Ann was convincing herself to feel more secure, more capable, than she really was. But he kept this thought to himself, said goodbye, and left her in the cave as he circled through the trees and up the slope, calling to the others.

"Hey!" he yelled when he spotted them in front of the Tower.

— *Sixteen* —

A LOOK INSIDE

I thought you were going to Thornton Falls," Zack said when he found not only Ruth and Ethan but also Miriam and their parents. It was so unusual to see everyone together at the Tower in the middle of the day like this, especially since Zack had thought he was alone with his father for the afternoon. Zack worried that perhaps something bad had happened.

"We were," his mother said, "but Ethan forgot his learner's permit, so we came back."

"I told everyone you'd gone outside," his father said.

"And we got kind of worried," Ethan said. "Dad said you left over an hour ago."

Zack calmed his breathing and looked at the five others before him. "So, you all came out here?" He glanced down the slope; for a moment, he wondered if Ann might appear.

"We did, Z," Miriam said gently. "Just to make sure you were okay."

"I'm not a baby," Zack said.

"No one thought that," his father said.

"All good, Zack," said Ruth. "Also, it gives Mom and Dad a chance to come to the Tower with us in the middle of the day."

Something felt off to Zack, and not just because his mother and his siblings had returned.

"Well, okay," Zack said hesitantly, "I'm fine. I was just exploring is all." No one said anything. "I'll head back home with you."

"Actually," their father said, "your mother and I asked the historical society if we could look inside. That's sort of why we're all here right now. I guess I got your brother and sisters out here under false pretenses." He pulled a key from his pocket. "The society let us have this extra key."

"We're going to go inside?" Ethan said. "Right now?" He looked to his siblings in astonishment, an expression they mirrored.

"What do you think, Deb?" their father said, looking at their mother. "Is now the right time?"

"Why not?" she said. "Let's take a look."

"I thought you had a ton of things to do in Thornton Falls," their father said, his tone playful.

"Dad!" Miriam said. "Let's take a look!"

"I'm with them," their mother said, turning to the kids.

Their father gave her a humorous look that seemed to say *I thought you were on my side*, and then he examined the others in turn.

"I guess if everyone's twisting my arm," he said wearily.

"You, father of the year," Ruth said. "How to make your children feel like today's the first day of Hanukkah."

Their father wheeled on her and began laughing as he said, "Okay, now you're taking it too far!" Everyone else laughed, too—including Zack—as their father reached the key toward the lock.

"I can't wait to see inside," Ethan said.

"Well, that's weird," their father said, a look of surprise on his face all of a sudden. He became still. "The door's already open. I didn't even put the key in, and it moved, I think."

"You must have pushed it a little," their mother said. She looked just as perplexed as their father.

"Maybe the people from the historical society left it unlocked accidentally," Ethan said.

"I suppose," their father said. "Still, it's kind of strange to think the place has been sitting open." He held up the key. "We didn't even need this."

Miriam pointed to the door. "Then I guess we should go in."

A moment later, inside the Tower, the six of them stood gaping at the marble floors and the statue-like faces around the rotunda and the greenish windows at the top level and the delicate designs on the railings and the graceful curve of the ceiling high above. Zack understood they all were overcome by the same wonder and amazement he'd felt when he'd first entered with Ann. For a long while—much longer than Zack would have guessed—no one spoke; they all simply stared up and around into every angle and corner of the place, and everyone stood in the muted emerald light. When they finally spoke, no one uttered anything louder than a whisper, and the sound echoed delicately through the broad space.

"This is incredible," their father said. "Beyond incredible."

"It's fantastic," their mother said, studying the main floor as if considering how best to decorate it.

"Those folks from the historical society have done a fantastic job in here," their father said. "You know, when you think about it, if the roof is secure and there haven't been any water leaks, I guess there's no reason anything should get out of order." He looked to the boarded-up windows. "Those are all secure, too. It really looks pretty good in here."

"Mom," Miriam said. "Dad. We have to try to open it back up. It's too amazing to keep it closed. Couldn't you talk to the historical society about it?"

"There would be some legal ground to cover first," their father said, "but maybe we can do something. This place is special."

"Up here," Ethan said as he began to climb the staircase. "To the top level."

"Look like how you remember it?" Ruth whispered to Zack.

He nodded eagerly. "Exactly," he said as Ruth took his hand and pulled him to the staircase to follow the others.

After ten minutes of looking around, the six Einsteins stood on the upper walkway—at the very same spot where Zack had stood with Ann—and examined the medallion at the center of the ceiling.

"That's what I read about online," Miriam said, pointing at the silver disk, and she explained once again what she had learned.

"Remember how the Bigelows were talking about the legend of this place?" Ethan said. "That medallion has to be part of it."

"Someone should write down what it says," their mother said.

"Good idea," Ruth agreed, giving Zack a sidelong glance. "And I just happen to have my journal, so I'll appoint myself scribe."

"Before you do," their father said, "can we all pause for just a moment?"

Everyone looked at him. Silence gathered in the Tower once again. Zack thought he felt the faintest caress of a breeze on his face, exactly as he had once before when he'd been in the Tower with Ann. It was so light, though, and so brief, he thought maybe he'd imagined it.

"What's on your mind, Mort?" their mother said; and right as she spoke, some bit of understanding registered on her face, and she nodded to her husband and then turned to the kids. She seemed to be looking to see if the door was open, as though she, too, had been touched by a breath of wind. Zack felt some ripple of awareness that didn't need to be spoken. He glanced at his siblings and felt certain they, too, had caught this same understanding, and that all of them—all six members of the family—had, almost in the same instant, been touched by the same feeling.

"Did you feel that?" Ethan said.

"I did," Miriam said softly.

"Me too," Ruth said.

"Can we say a few words for Susan?" their father said, putting a hand to his cheek as if to capture the brush of the breeze on it.

"You read my mind," their mother said.

A long silence followed as everyone looked around—to see who might go first or, perhaps, to discover from which corner of the Tower the now-stilled wind had arisen—and then Ruth said, "Susan, Susan, I wish you were here with us right now to see this beautiful place. We love you."

"I miss you, Susan," Miriam said. "Every day. Every day I'm thinking about you."

"Me too," Ethan said. "I miss your little hugs and all the cute things you used to say. I'd give anything to have you back."

Their mother put her head down and pressed a hand to her forehead. Zack thought she was about to cry. "Have mercy upon her, and shelter her soul in the shadow of thy wings," she said softly, reciting a line from a prayer Zack recalled. She looked up. "I loved our little girl. I don't really know the full prayer, but I always liked those words. Susan would have liked them, too."

Their father glanced up at the medallion and then out into the open space of the Tower. "We love you, Susan. We'll never, ever forget you." He looked at the others and gave two heavy taps on his chest. "Right here," he said. "We keep her right here."

Everyone waited in silence for a moment, giving Zack space to speak if he wanted.

"Maybe if we fix up the Tower and say that charm," Zack said, "everything will be all right. Everything. Like it was." He spoke quickly, breathlessly, and he moved his gaze from one person to the next; but no one said a word. Zack glanced through the small square of clear window beside him—he stood back from the cluster the others had formed, and he was the only one with a view out the window. He saw Ann walking quickly across the broad field in front and just east of the Tower. Zack watched as she entered the forest.

"Do you see something, Zack?" his mother said.

He pointed to the window. "There's a girl I ran into who lives around here," he said. "I just saw her."

Ruth scooted over beside him and peered out the window; she turned quickly back to the others and gave a shrug right as Miriam moved to take a look herself.

"I don't see anything, Z," Miriam said.

"She was just there," Zack said. "Ann is her name. She went into the trees, so that's why you can't see her."

"This is a girl you met?" their father said. "She lives in the area?"

"On the other side of the woods," Zack said. He looked to his brother and sisters—one part of him wanted them to confirm that he'd already mentioned Ann, because he felt this would prove something definite to his parents; but another part of him wanted them to remain silent about Ann, as they'd promised. "She lives with her mother. Her father died in a war."

"In a war?" their mother said. She pinched up her face and looked at her husband before examining Zack once more. "How did you meet this girl again?"

"I saw her by the woods one day," Zack said. "She was just walking around. She's lived here since she was little, and her mom lets her go out on her own."

"Well, how old is this girl, Zack?" his father said. "I mean, this is all news to us."

"She's nine," he said. "And she kind of looks like Susan."

Zack wanted to say something more, wanted to add some detail that would clarify things and make the others see how simple it all was: He'd met a girl who was very independent and familiar with the area. He couldn't tell them everything, of course, about how the two of them had been in the Tower together twice, or how Ann had shown him the cave on the slope below and the circle of trees and Orland Wetherill's cabin, and how they'd decided to solve the mystery of the medallion together if they could. But he felt he'd told them enough.

The look on his father's face suggested otherwise. "Zack, I want to ask you this again, and I want you to tell me the truth. You say you met a girl around the area, and you don't know where she lives, and she's the same age as Susan and looks like her, too? Do I have that right? And no one else has met her or seen her?"

Zack's stomach dropped. "You think I'm making her up," he said, with no hint of question in his voice. He felt resigned to being disbelieved.

"Your father didn't say that," his mother said. "We're just trying to understand more about your friend."

Zack sighed as he glanced out the window once again. He kept his eyes focused on the part of the forest in which Ann had disappeared. And then a thought came to him like a spark of light in the darkness. "Her mother works at a restaurant on the highway," he said, looking to his father. Something about this fact felt persuasive beyond any doubt—he was certain the others would believe him now, because this particular detail felt like something he couldn't possibly have made up. "The Double-R Café," he said. "She's a waitress."

"Zack," his father said, his voice so quiet and steady and somber that Zack was afraid of what was coming next. "Your mother and I—all of us, actually—have driven on that highway enough times to be pretty familiar with it." He hesitated. "There's no place called the Double-R Café."

Zack felt dizzy. He put a hand on the railing and stared at his father.

"I'm sorry," his father said. "It's the truth. You can check for yourself." He looked to Deborah and the kids, and then back at Zack. "I know this isn't easy to hear," he said, "but I want you to give some thought to what I'm about to say, because there are really only two possibilities here: Either your friend is kind of bending the truth a bit, or maybe—just maybe—your friend is, actually, the sort of friend you used to have when you were little." He paused again. "You know what I mean, I think."

Zack kept his hand on the railing and didn't look up. "She's real," he said. "I know she is. I know what you're all thinking, but she's real."

After a moment, Miriam moved past Zack and Ruth and headed for the stairs.

"Maybe we should get going, Mom," she said. "I still need those new basketball sneakers."

Miriam stepped heavily down the stairs. The others followed, and Zack remained standing for a moment before joining them. He was the last one out as they departed the Tower; but just before his father closed the doors, Zack peered at the medallion high above and thought about Ann's words in the cave when the two of them had been discussing it, about the things she'd said about the number nine.

One of Nine, he thought, though he felt so confused about what had just happened inside the Tower, he wondered if the mystery of the medallion might be impossible to solve.

— *Seventeen* —

THE LIGHTS, AGAIN

The next evening after sundown, the four kids were back on the stairs of the Tower, admiring the night sky. Zack hadn't said a word to his father for a full day, and he hadn't discussed Ann with his siblings since then, either. He'd remained aloof the entire time; but when Ethan invited him to come learn more about the constellations by the Tower, Zack decided to join.

"Okay, what's that one?" Ruth asked Ethan, who, once again, was pointing out various clusters of stars to the others.

"Leo," Ethan said. "The lion. The easiest way to find it is by following a line from the top two stars in the cup of the Big Dipper, and then you come to that group that looks like a backward question mark."

"I don't see a lion in there," Miriam said.

"You have to use your imagination, Mir," Ethan said. "The

lion's body kind of stretches back from the stars I just mentioned."

"Still," Miriam said. "I don't know. That's a lot of imagination."

"They're stars!" Ruth said. "What do you expect?"

"If you join the troop, Z," Ethan said, "you can come with me to camp next summer. That's where I learned all of this."

Zack knew that as much as Ethan wanted to jump right back into scouting, it had turned out he was just too busy settling into life in Vista Point and helping around the house to arrange things. Ethan had decided to join a new troop once school resumed; he'd mentioned several times that he hoped Zack would join with him.

"I might," Zack said. For years, as he'd watched his brother advance through the scouting ranks and learn about the outdoors and go on hikes and camping trips, Zack had been looking forward to emulating Ethan and becoming a scout. It had always seemed like the perfect way to bring to life the adventures he'd read about in his books.

"You *might*?" Miriam said. "I thought you were looking forward to becoming a scout."

Zack didn't answer, and in the darkness it was impossible to see the others' faces; but he sensed Ruth giving Miriam a look to make her stop pursuing the subject.

Ethan rapped his knuckles on the big piece of plywood covering the window opening closest to them.

"Can you guys believe Mom and Dad want to open this place back up?" he said. "It'll be incredible."

Following the visit everyone had made the day before, their parents had informed the kids they'd decided to inquire with the historical society about assuming ownership of the Tower and attempting some restoration work on it.

"Frankly, the place is in pretty good shape," their father had said over Shabbat dinner the night before. "The folks at the historical society have told us they would consider letting us own the place if we took over the upkeep. We're going to give it some serious thought, but at a minimum, I think we should try to fix it up in time for Labor Day. The society has given us permission to do that, at least for now, and they'll even pay for some of the materials."

"The windows are the main thing," their mother had said, "but the company we hired to fix the house is really good with that kind of work, so we might have gotten lucky."

"We could help with any of the cleaning or straightening-up inside," Miriam volunteered. She and the others had already talked it over.

"I think we'd only need an inspection by the county," their father said, "and then turn the water back on and clear out the road and parking area a bit. It just might be doable, especially with help from all of you."

Now the four kids were beside the Tower itself, the mid-July night had turned black, and they were all considering Ethan's words.

"Can you imagine how great it will be to have sightseers come up here all the time?" Ruth said. "They'll probably check out our place, too, so it will be good for business." She cleared her throat. *"The Einsteins never imagined their humble little inn would become the site of the world's most famous international poetry conference, but that's exactly what—"*

"You are losing it, Ruth!" Miriam said with a laugh.

"I think it must mean they're not worried about Horatio anymore," Ethan said. "I mean, if they're thinking about owning the Tower, that has to mean there's no problem from the county with moving ahead on the bed-and-breakfast."

Zack had been considering this exact point for the past day, and Ethan's logic made a lot of sense.

"I agree," Miriam said. "On the other hand, maybe they figure even if they can't open up the bed-and-breakfast when they planned, at least people will come up here to see the Tower."

"But we're not going to charge people to come to the Tower," Ruth said. "I mean, are we?"

"No, I just mean it could be a way for Mom and Dad to show they want to be good members of the community," Miriam said. "I guess. I don't know. I think Ethan's right, though."

"What do you think, Zack?" Ethan said.

Zack was sitting on the Tower's stairs and trying to identify a couple of the constellations Ethan had explained, even while he listened to the others.

"About that man Horatio?" Zack said. He wasn't sure what he thought about him. The man had been intimidating when he'd harangued the family that one morning, but the story of his life—losing his wife and daughter, in particular—had been so saddening that Zack found he felt sorry for him. "I don't want him to cause any problems for us," Zack said. "But I sort of hope he can stop being mad about everything."

No one spoke for a moment.

"You are a good guy, Z," Miriam said. "Seriously."

"I was thinking something else, too," Zack said. "What if when we open up the Tower, it could be a place where people could show their art and things like that?"

It was an idea he'd borrowed from one of the Falcons and Bandits books, where the kids in the story organize their own art exhibit. But the fact was, over the preceding week Zack had found himself thinking often of the banners he'd seen when the four of them had come across the camp in the woods. He'd been captivated by the swirl of shapes they held and the interesting designs. The idea of displaying them—of making the Tower a place where artists from the area could show their work—had slowly settled in his head as an appealing possibility, something his mother and father might find attractive.

"That's a great idea," Ruth said. "Like our own artists colony! That's what they call it in all the old books about writers and painters."

"It's actually not a bad idea," Miriam said. "There's a lot of people around here who make crafts and things. I bet Mom and Dad would go for it."

"I was thinking of it after we saw those banners around the cabins in the woods," Zack said.

"*Ruth Einstein was pleased to be appointed the leader of a diverse community of writers and artists at Vista Point's world-famous Tower,*" Ruth said.

"The night air is messing with your head, Ruth," Ethan said.

"Hey, hey, hey!" Miriam said with an urgency that sounded disconnected from the fun everyone was having. She bolted upright in something like panic. "Look!"

"The light!" Ruth said, and the attention of all four kids was riveted by the flashing of a powerful beam from far across the river, just as they'd seen weeks before.

"Here, here," Ethan said, fumbling in his pocket for the flashlight he'd brought. Ruth was prepared, too, and whipped out her journal and a pen as Miriam moved to them, took the flashlight from Ethan, and held the light on Ruth's page. They'd worked out this plan three weeks before and had brought the flashlight with them on each subsequent nighttime visit to the Tower; and now, it seemed, they would be able to document what they were seeing.

"We missed the first few flashes," Ethan said. "Let's write down what we can. Remember how it works. A quick flash is a dot, a longer shine of light is a dash, and if they stop everything for a moment, that's a space between letters. A longer stop is a space between words." He stood staring at the light; Zack moved beside him as Ethan called out what he saw, and Ruth wrote it all down.

"Dash. Space. Dot, dot, dot, dot. Space. Dot. Long space. That's the end of a word," Ethan said, and he continued detailing the flashes. It went on for not quite three minutes, and then all became dark again.

"Hey," Miriam said as they stood and waited to see if anything more would come. "I just realized something. It's ten o'clock on a Saturday night. That's exactly when we saw the lights last time. Day of the week and time."

"You're right," Ethan said. "That must be the pattern."

"We went to a movie one Saturday," Ruth said, "and we didn't come out here last Saturday, so we haven't been back on a Saturday night since the first time."

"Look," Ruth said. "Everyone." She sat on the stairs, and the three others huddled beside her to examine her sheet of paper.

"It repeats," Zack said as he stared at the symbols on the page. He was completely unfamiliar with Morse code, but something about the pattern of dots and dashes on the paper seemed to leap out at him. "Right there." He pointed to a spot in the several lines of jottings where, it was clear, the marks began repeating what Ruth had written at the top of her page.

"The person must have run through the message twice, just in case," Miriam said. "How did you notice that, Zack?"

"I just did. I don't know."

"So the message by itself is right here," Ruth said, drawing a box around the following marks:

-.-. .-. --- ... ... / - .... . / -... .-. .. -.. --. . / ... .- . -. - .... /
.... --- ..- ... . / .-- . ... -

"I put a slash whenever you said *new word*, Ethan," Ruth added.

"Six words," Ethan said. "The person sent six words."

"That's a pretty good system," Ruth said. And at the mention of that word—*system*—Zack felt something electric go through him.

"Morse code is incredible," Ethan said. "I just wish I'd brought my decoder grid with me. It's in my Boy Scout handbook in my room."

Miriam stood. "Then what are we waiting for? We need to go home and figure out what this says. Come on!"

She turned and dashed off into the darkness, and before Zack knew it, he, Ethan, and Ruth were following, aiming for the bright windows of their house far ahead.

System, Zack kept hearing in his head. And then, even as he ran through the darkness, he remembered where he'd heard that word before: *My father taught me a system*, Ann had said.

The four kids reached the house, nearly knocking the rear door down as they barged inside to find their parents sitting quietly in the living room and reading.

"We saw the lights again!" Ruth called, and Ethan barreled up the stairs to his room to get his handbook while the others gathered around the table to learn the secret of the flashing lights.

Eighteen

THE HOUSE ACROSS THE RIVER

"*ross the bridge seventh house west,*" their mother repeated.

It had taken several minutes and a few instances of guess-work, given a bit of confused transcription ("I just wrote down what you said!" Ruth protested when Ethan told her something might be wrong) to work things through, all while using the decoder from Ethan's handbook:

A •–	H ••••	O –––	V •••–
B –•••	I ••	P •––•	W •––
C –•–•	J •–––	Q ––•–	X –••–
D –••	K –•–	R •–•	Y –•––
E •	L •–••	S •••	Z ––••
F ••–•	M ––	T –	
G ––•	N –•	U ••–	

Once everything had been sorted out, though, the message sent from the other side of the river was: *Cross the bridge seventh house west.*

It didn't make complete sense to any of them, though the message apparently suggested that if a person took the bridge across the Grand River, turned west on the road that paralleled the river, and then looked for the seventh house along it, the source of the light might be located. And so now, after a fitful night's rest by all six of the Einsteins, they were packed into their Subaru and speeding north across the bridge to the other side of the river.

They'd waited until eleven in the morning ("It's Sunday, after all," their father had said), and then they'd headed out. The day was bright and hot already, the water of the river was nearly as blue as the sky, and the forested slopes on either side of the Grand looked very steep and foreboding. Zack glanced behind him through the rear window and could make out the Tower high up on the bluff, standing like the isolated battlement of a castle. It looked stark against the pure blue of the sky, and he realized once again just how high above the river it stood. He pictured Ann perched on its stairs—maybe at that very moment—and staring far down at the bridge to see the car he was in gliding silently away to the far side of the water. As they'd driven on the highway beside the river and east to the bridge, Zack had kept an eye out, hoping to see the Double-R Café.

"*Cross the bridge seventh house west,*" their mother said again midspan on the bridge.

"Quite a mystery," their father said.

"I'm just wondering what in the world we're going to find," their mother said. It was exactly what Zack had been thinking; he was certain everyone in the car had been mulling the same thing, too.

"Is everything still on track to open by Labor Day?" Miriam said.

"What brings that up?" their father said.

"When we were at the Tower last night," Ethan said, "we just started talking about, you know, how that man came over that one day and said he was going to try to stop us from opening."

"You haven't really said too much about it since then," Ruth said. "So we were wondering."

Their parents exchanged a pensive glance, and an uncomfortable silence filled the car.

"I guess there's still a problem," Miriam said.

"What makes you say that?" their mother said.

"When you look at each other that way," Miriam said, "it means you don't want to tell us something."

"Mir," their father said, his tone slightly weary, "we're working it through, okay? There actually might be a little snag, an old statute that guy Horatio found that no one knew about and that no one ever would have known about if he hadn't pressed the issue. But I'm confident this will all be a tiny bump in the road that we'll put behind us."

"In a few years," their mother said, "when we have the very best bed-and-breakfast up and down the river, we won't even remember this complication."

"Zack had a great idea that we should have local artists display their stuff at the Tower," Ethan said.

Their parents looked at each other again, and their mother said, "That's an intriguing idea." She arched her eyebrows in genuine interest. "I like it."

"So do I," said their father. "That would add a lot of appeal to the place. A real community feel."

"Those people out in the woods had some cool flags at their place," Miriam said.

"They weren't flags," Ruth said. "Flags are for countries. They were banners."

"Well, you know what I mean," Miriam said. "I'm just saying, I bet a lot of people in the area would want to show their art."

"All good back there, Zack?" their father said, glancing in the rearview mirror.

Zack was glad to hear that his idea had been well received, though he wasn't focused on the possible opening of the Tower just then or whether it might be a place where artists could gather. He was, instead, beyond eager to find out where the message of the flashing lights was going to lead; he also couldn't stop thinking about Ann telling him on several occasions how drawn she was to the Tower and that her father had worked out some system for communicating with her. It all seemed connected somehow, but he couldn't make sense of it.

"I just wonder what we're going to find at the seventh house," Zack said.

"We all are," his father said. "That's one thing I can say for sure. We all are."

The car reached the end of the bridge, and then the road continued up and into the trees before it came to a T; their father turned left—west—along the one-lane road that ran through the dense forest.

"Let's keep track of things, everyone," he said. "I guess we just count off the number of houses or driveways we find along the way."

The road that followed the river on this side was much narrower and saw much less traffic than the highway across the water, and so there were hardly any cars the Einsteins had to be concerned with as they moved slowly westward through the tall trees.

"First house, right there," Ethan said, pointing into the hemlocks where a small dirt lane led off.

"Looks like there are only turnoffs to single residences over here," their mother said, "so that should make our job easier."

"And they're spread out, too," Ruth said.

"There's the second house," Miriam said.

It took about five minutes of driving—with everyone in the car tallying the houses along the road as they went—before they came to the seventh turnoff.

"I think we're here," their father said, pointing north—up into the stand of fir and hemlock—along the rutted lane that turned off from the road. "Number seven."

Zack glanced southward through the trees; the Tower, which was just visible through an obscuring grid of branches, was tiny against the horizon far atop the bluff on the other side of the river, and it stood almost directly opposite the spot where the car sat idling.

Everyone in the Subaru peered up the lane, though there was little to see because the trees were so thick. And then their father turned onto the lane and drove ahead through two bends in the roadway. A log cabin came into view just as three large German shepherds came bounding toward the car and barking furiously, causing everyone to raise the open windows of the car to half height.

The cabin, with a listing stone chimney and a steeply sloped metal roof that looked like it had been dinged several times by falling branches, seemed very old. This was partly because moss clung to it in the cracks here and there, and it appeared to have water stains near the foundation; but it was also because there was so much junk surrounding it: rotted lumber, two rusted lawn mowers, a moldy sofa with exposed springs, broken chairs and bookcases, and a small mountain of cans and bottles. A grimy propane tank stood off to one side, and all sorts of hoses and lines were sprawled around it. Something that looked like a storage shed—or maybe an outhouse, Zack thought—stood behind the tank and close to the edge of the forest, which looked particularly thick and dark where the house's clearing ended.

"This place looks terrible," Miriam said.

"I don't think we'll get to experience it close up with those dogs out there," their father said. "But, yeah, it looks pretty rough here."

"Perhaps we're in the wrong place," their mother said.

"It's definitely the seventh house," Ethan said. "But I wish it wasn't." He paused as the dogs leaped at the car, barking ferociously. "Maybe we should turn around, Dad."

"*The psychotic criminal had the Einstein family right where he wanted them*—" Ruth began, but their mother cut her off.

"Don't do that right now, Ruth," she said. "It's not funny. This is serious." She put a hand on her husband's shoulder. "Maybe we should turn around. This doesn't feel right."

"Look," Zack said, pointing to the cabin. "Someone's coming out."

Everyone stared at the cabin door as it angled open; the astonishment in the car multiplied tenfold when all the Einsteins realized they recognized the man stepping into the yard: Horatio Cuvallo.

"You've got to be kidding me," their father said. "Him? Here?"

"Dad, let's go," Ruth said. "We should get out of here right now."

Horatio began yelling something in their direction and gesticulating with both hands; he was scowling, and he wore only a white T-shirt under his suspenders, along with his jeans and boots. Zack had the distinct feeling the family had woken him from a nap.

It was impossible to hear what Horatio was saying. He was too far away, the car windows were only half open, and the dogs were barking loudly, but then Horatio yelled something, and the three German shepherds stopped their bounding and pawing and trotted back to him.

"At least he called off the hounds," Miriam said.

Horatio stood just a few feet in front of the cabin, and the dogs paced before him. He squinted at the car, and then he lifted his chin as if he suddenly realized who was in his yard.

"What do you want?" he yelled. "What are you doing out here?"

Their father rolled his window all the way down. "Good morning, Mr. Cuvallo."

"Nice, Dad," Miriam said under her breath. "Now let's go."

"Mir, quit!" Ethan said.

"What do you want?" Horatio called, even louder this time, his voice gruffer. "This is my place, and you're trespassing!"

"My kids saw some lights flashing last night when they were up on the bluff near our house," their father said.

Zack became aware of the ticking of the car as it idled; the noise was a lulling vibration that made him think of the way he sometimes felt at the Tower. He was tense with expectation, waiting to see what would come next. The cabin looked so run-down, it made Zack feel awful—the Bigelows' cabin had been welcoming and quaint, but this place looked unpleasant and unhappy, and Zack suddenly hoped his father would get them away from it as soon as he could. Zack put a hand to his pants pocket, felt the outline of his arrowhead.

Horatio's face went blank. He looked confused, as though the explanation the kids' father had given had been the last thing he'd expected to hear.

"What's that got to do with me?" Horatio said, composing himself, his angry expression returning, though his voice had thinned a bit.

"They wrote down the flashes of light," their father continued. "And it was in Morse code. The message told us to come out here, the seventh house to the west after you cross the bridge. So here we are. And we're about as surprised to see you as I think you are to see us. Of course, we're wondering why you sent the message and what it's all about."

Again, Horatio looked absolutely startled. He turned to the dogs and lifted an arm in a gesture that indicated displeasure or annoyance, as if he might strike one of them or simply wanted them to move away. It was apparent to Zack that Horatio didn't want to explain anything.

He peered at the car. "I don't have any idea what you're talking about, but you need to get off my property. Right now."

"Why were you flashing those lights?" Miriam yelled. "We saw them once before, too!"

"Miriam!" their mother said. "Stop that!"

Horatio glared at the car, and then his expression became something that looked mocking, as if he was glad the Einsteins were flustered.

"Well, it certainly is curious," their father called to Horatio, continuing the thread of his explanation to him. "Someone flashing those lights right from this spot, and a message spelling out to come here. Something's definitely going on, that's for sure."

"I don't know what you're getting at," Horatio called. "If I were you, I'd be a little more concerned about your legal issues rather than running around on a Sunday morning trespassing on people's property."

"There aren't any Keep Out signs," Ethan said, but quietly, so that only the members of his family could hear.

"Mr. Cuvallo," their father said, "we know things haven't always gone easy for you, but there's really no reason for you to be put out with us. We have no quarrel with you."

"You've had a quarrel with me from the moment you set foot on that property up there that should still be mine," Horatio called. "And you're gonna keep having a quarrel with me because the county's gonna shut you down." He pointed toward the road. "Now leave."

"Why are you so angry?" Miriam called through her half-open window.

Their mother turned to scowl at her, but almost immediately all eyes were focused on Horatio beside his cabin. He stood with his hand in the air still, pointing, looking almost like a statue. For a moment it seemed as if his face might soften, as though he might take back all his harsh words and give up his rage. It looked, almost, as though he might answer Miriam. Instead, he kept his arm stationary, lowered his brow in doubled fury, and yelled, "Leave!"

Their father reversed the car, angled back, and then curved onto the rutted dirt lane and away from Horatio's cabin. No one said a word as they turned onto the road and then headed straight for the bridge across which they'd traveled not fifteen minutes before. By what seemed some unspoken agreement, everyone remained silent until they reached the south side—their side—of the divide, and then their father pulled over to the shoulder and turned off the car. A feeling of relief came over Zack, as though he and his family had escaped some terrible danger.

"That was scary," Ruth said. "I'll admit it. That man is scary."

"He definitely was the one flashing the light, though," Ethan said. "Did you see his face when Dad asked him about it? He knew we'd figured it out."

"It's just that we don't know anything more now than we did before we went out there," their father said.

"Well," their mother said, "we know he's committed to seeing us fail. As if that wasn't clear already." She looked at Miriam. "I wish you hadn't said anything to him. It just got him going."

"Well, he was yelling at us, Mom," Miriam said with irritation.

"We don't need to yell back at him," their mother said, and Miriam slumped in her seat. "Seriously. It just makes everything worse."

"I think he wants to find someone," Zack said. "Or he wants someone to find him." He wasn't sure why this thought had come to him, but there had been something so desperate—and sad— about Horatio that Zack couldn't help thinking he'd been moved to flash the light out of some deep distress. "Right?" Zack added. "I mean, wouldn't that be the reason for sending a signal like that?"

"In the middle of the night?" Ruth said. "Out in the middle of nowhere? I'm sorry, Zack, but I think the guy is just super confused and angry. Or he's doing it on purpose to mess with our heads. I don't know."

"I'm actually more committed now than before to opening our place *and* the Tower by Labor Day," their father said as he restarted the car. "I'm not going to let that man intimidate us."

"You, committed bed-and-breakfast owner," Miriam said. "How to make sure a man in an old cabin with three wild dogs doesn't slow you down."

Their mother put a hand to her forehead and began to laugh. "Okay," she said, "this has been a very strange morning. I'll put some lunch on when we get home, and then we can get back to work."

"Labor Day, here we come!" their father said, and he pulled back onto the road. "The Vista Point Bed-and-Breakfast will be open for business!"

— *Nineteen* —

A STARTLING STORY

One and a half weeks passed. The kids visited the Tower (though not the inside—their father insisted that an official inspection needed to be done before any cleanup could begin) nearly every day and spent hours scrubbing the outside of it to clear the mildew that had built up. They helped with laying carpet and hanging curtains and arranging furniture in the upstairs bedrooms of the house. They went swimming at the pools by the waterfalls four times, and Zack even convinced Ethan and Ruth to revisit the cabin with him once, where they all "discovered" the plaque with the words *The ninth is one* on it. They continued hiking the trails all around; and they even waited at the Tower at ten o'clock on the Saturday night following the one on which they'd deciphered the coded message, and, sure enough, they saw the lights flashing out the same words once again, something that surprised them greatly.

Zack still passed many hours of each day alone in his room—he made it through the next three books in the Falcons and Bandits series: *Sparrow Spot*, *We Never Intended to Set Sail*, and *Hidden Lake*—though he found that life at Vista Point was prompting him to spend more time with his siblings. He kept an eye out for Ann daily, even visiting the cave to leave her notes (which were never answered and, it seemed, never seen) and straying into the forest on his own in the hope of finding her; but, almost two weeks after he'd last seen her, she still hadn't appeared. He studied his note, too, the one on which he'd written the strange lines from the medallion; and he and his brother and sisters discussed it on several occasions.

"I thought at first it might be a substitution cipher," Ethan said on one occasion as the four kids dried off beside the water of the upper pool after a swim. "I have a grid on that in my scouting handbook. It's where, like, every time you have an *A*, you replace it with another letter, and then the same thing for *B*, and so on. But nothing works."

"That would be too simple," Miriam said. "It's way more complicated than that."

"If it's a really tough substitution cipher," Ethan said, "we'd have no chance of figuring it out. That's what I'm worried about."

"But it can't be impossible," Ruth said. "Remember that thing you read us by Orland Wetherill, Mir, where he said people should keep the answer to themselves? That must mean we can solve it."

"But that doesn't mean it's easy," Miriam said.

"Still," Ruth said, "it can't be all *that* hard, right? We're missing something obvious."

"The number nine is the key," Zack said. "It's on the medallion, on the cabin, on the tombstone."

"You're probably right," Miriam said. "I was even trying to shift everything nine places. Like every *A* would become…" She paused to count letters in her head. "…an *I*, or maybe a *J*, depending on how you count it out. But that didn't work."

"I tried taking every ninth letter and putting them in order," Ethan said, "but that didn't work, either. Right away it turned into something that didn't make any sense."

"We've been over all this before," Ruth said. "We're missing something." She looked to Zack. "Any brainstorms come to you lately?"

"Nothing," he said. "But I'm positive there's something to do with the number nine, and when we figure it out, we'll be, like, wow, we should have seen that already."

Zack was definitely stumped, and the puzzle nagged at him as he went about his days. Before he knew it, though, the end of July was fast approaching, and he found himself thinking that he would begin at a new school in just over a month. This worried him, not only because he was anxious about fitting in and meeting new kids, but also because it made the move to Vista Point seem fixed: There was no going back to Roseburg, and every time this notion came to him, he felt a twinge of desperation for Susan. One night, Zack had woken up feeling so terrible about his sister, he'd gone to his parents' room and begun crying. His mother had held him, told him over and over that he wasn't to blame for anything; but Zack was never convinced by these words, never consoled.

"You're a good person, Zack," his mother and father would say. "You didn't do anything wrong."

Why don't they see? Zack thought as he considered all the things inside him that were confusing and all the times he was selfish or thoughtless or hurtful. *That* person must be the real one underneath everything else, he felt; *that* person must be the one who didn't keep an eye on Susan. *How can they not see that?* Zack thought.

When school began, he believed, the life his family had left behind would truly be gone forever.

Very early on the final Thursday of July, Zack was lying on his bed reading *The Enormous Five*, the ninth book in the Falcons and Bandits series, when he noticed someone stepping out of the forest east of the Tower. He jumped off his bed and pressed his face to the window: Ann, once again, was walking across the field. She glanced at the house, and Zack felt certain she was hoping he saw her.

He waved frantically, but the distance was too great for her to spot him, and then she disappeared beneath the slope of the hill just beyond the Tower. Zack waited a moment to see if she would reappear; and when she didn't, he put on his shoes, went downstairs as quietly as he could, and—not finding anyone up and about yet—slipped silently out the back door. The air was still cool, and there was dew on the grass.

Zack took the most direct route into the trees nearest the house so that he wouldn't be seen, and once he was within the protective cover of the forest, he took off at a run, heading for the slope where it rolled away from the woods. He had a notion to call out to Ann as he drew closer, but he thought better of this and held back.

After he was clear of the trees and had run downhill a ways, he angled back so that he could approach the Tower directly and remain out of sight from the house; and just as the stairs of the stone building came into view, Zack saw Ann sitting on them and looking as though she'd been waiting for him to arrive.

"Hey!" she called. "It's you!"

"Where've you been?" Zack said through heavy puffs of breath as he came up to her. He stopped, his chest heaving. "I haven't seen you in so long."

"I know," Ann said. "We went away for over a week." She stood abruptly and glanced across the river. "My mom had to go help my aunt in Roseburg, so she couldn't work at the café."

There was so much Zack wanted to ask, he wasn't sure where to start.

"You were in Roseburg?" he said. "Is your aunt okay?"

"She's fine. We go stay with her sometimes."

Zack was already very uncertain about Ann's explanations, but he was glad to see she was all right. He had been starting to wonder if some problem—maybe something serious—had arisen that had made it impossible for her to come see him.

"The place where your mom works," Zack said. "It's called the Double-R Café?"

"Yes." She squinted at Zack. "The Double-R."

Zack took a seat on the stairs as he let out a final long breath; he felt he'd gotten his air back finally. "My dad says there's no place on the highway with that name."

Ann sat, too, and pinched her face in perplexity. "It's where my mother works."

"Can I ask you something?"

"Yes."

Zack had thought he wanted to ask her straight-out if she lived in the woods with the people in the cabins; he wanted to let her know that she didn't need to be shy about telling him the truth, that there was no reason for her to hide this from him. But right as he began to speak the words, he stopped himself: He hadn't seen her for many days, they were at the Tower together once again, and he realized he didn't want to put her on the spot.

"Have you ever been to the other side of the river?" was the question he found himself asking her.

"I have," Ann said. "Across the bridge."

"We went there last week," Zack said. "It's kind of hard to explain, but there was a guy flashing a light at us here by the Tower really late one night, and the flashes spelled out letters in a code. It's called Morse code, if you haven't heard of it. Anyway, the message he was flashing told us where to go on the other side of the river, so we went there and met him, and it turned out he was this mean old man who came to our house once trying to scare my parents."

Ann was staring intently at Zack as he told his story; she said nothing when he concluded, simply continued looking at him as though she couldn't believe what he'd said.

"What's the matter?" Zack asked.

"I do know about Morse code," Ann said. "That's the system my father told me about. Remember? The thing I told you once?"

A shiver ran through Zack. "That's what your father taught you?"

"Well, he explained it to me, mostly. There was that story I told you, how I was scared about getting lost in the woods, so my father showed me how he could flash a light where you go short light and long light, and he said the flashes added up to letters in Morse code. He even used to play it with me in the house. We'd turn off the lights and make it dark, and he would get a flashlight and make those signals at me, and then I would sound them out. Like, short, long, short, short, long, long, and keep going. He gave me a little card that had an alphabet on it with the long and short lines next to each letter. That way I could understand that code."

Zack felt so stunned by this, he wasn't sure what to make of it. There was something beyond coincidence going on here, he was sure, but he couldn't think what it might be. How in the world could Horatio Cuvallo and his flashing lights have anything to do with Ann?

"But even if you knew the whole system," Zack said, "and you and your dad practiced it, or he taught you about it, how would that help you if you got lost?"

"Don't you remember what I told you?"

"What?"

"About coming to this stone building? He told me to come here if I got lost. This is the most famous place around, and you can see it from everywhere. He told me to come here, and he would flash the lights."

Zack felt so agitated, he stood and began glancing around. He felt as though there might be something to see or something to understand; but instead, all remained silent aside from the hum, the vibration, the tiny buzz of things that seemed to exist somewhere at the back of everything around Zack and Ann and the Tower.

"How could you see a light here, though?" Zack said, picturing Ann just as she was now, sitting beside the Tower in daylight. The notion that she would be here as he and his siblings had come—in the darkness—seemed impossible. How would a young girl, all alone, find her way to this spot after dark?

"No one could see any lights at all," he said. "It's too bright."

"He told me to come here at night," Ann said quietly. "I remember what he said."

Zack felt the breath go out of him; he stared at Ann, waiting for her to continue.

"*Ten o'clock on a Saturday night, at the stone building just look for the light,*" she said, a singsong chant that sounded so simple, so sincere—and yet described so exactly the flashing lights that had come from Horatio Cuvallo—that Zack had to sit once again.

"That's what he told me," Ann said. "That little poem. So I could remember it."

"We saw that light," Zack said. "Every Saturday at ten o'clock, he flashes it. He's looking for you."

"Who?"

"Ann, tell me something. The truth, okay? Are you living with those people in the woods?"

"What do you mean? I live with my mother. We have a house. I don't live in the woods."

"But is that story about the lights…did someone tell you

about it? It wasn't really your own father who told you about it, right?"

Ann peered at Zack as though she couldn't understand the words he was saying. "I don't know why you're asking me all these things. My father taught me about the code for the lights, and he told me to come here if I got lost."

Zack stared right back at Ann and tried to fit her words into everything else swirling through his mind; and as he looked at her, a distressing thought came to him: Ann was lying.

"I wish you would tell me the truth," he said.

Ann's shoulders slumped, and she averted her eyes, looking to the patchy grass that grew just beyond where the stairs ended before the Tower. She sat that way for a moment, and Zack thought she must be making up her mind to be honest with him, to tell him she'd heard the story of the lights and the Tower and all of it from someone, and it had seemed fun or thrilling to think about herself being part of it—but that it really had nothing to do with her.

She stood. "I'd better get home," she said softly.

"Wait," Zack said, standing as well. "Don't leave. I was just wondering about everything you were saying. That's all."

"I'd better get going." She turned away from him and began walking.

Zack held out a hand, even though Ann's back was to him, and he was about to say something—but he remained silent and watched her walk slowly toward the woods. A feeling of desolation came over him as she stepped into the dense cover of trees, something that reminded Zack of that night at the fair with Susan; and he wondered if, just now, he should have said something or done something to keep Ann from leaving.

He lost sight of her.

— *Twenty* —

LUNCH AND A LETTER

Zack?" came a voice from behind him, and Zack turned to see Miriam standing and looking at him.

"Hey," he said. He was rattled, but he tried to make his voice sound as ordinary as possible.

"What's up?" she said, coming to him. "Why are you out here so early by yourself?"

He turned away from Miriam and pointed toward the woods. "Didn't you see her?"

"Who?" Miriam looked past Zack in the direction he was pointing. She tilted her head in perplexity, and Zack heard the familiar note of mistrust entering her voice. "I didn't see anyone."

"It was Ann," Zack said. "The girl I told you about. She was just here. You had to have seen her."

Miriam shook her head. "I just came out here because Ruth

said she thought she saw you leave the house. She didn't think it was a big deal, but I wanted to check. So I came out to see if you were over this way." Miriam looked to the woods again. "I didn't see anyone else, though." She took a few more steps toward Zack. "It's just you here, Z. No one else."

"She was here. I was talking to her."

"Zack," Miriam said insistently. "You need to think about what Dad said. Remember?"

"I'm not making it up."

Miriam cast her arms out to either side in a gesture that said *How can I believe you when there's nothing here to see?*

"I'm not lying," Zack said.

"I know you feel bad, Zack. We all do. But you need to try to deal with it."

"You want me to just forget everything?" he said, his voice coming high and tight and his eyes beginning to water. "Forget about Susan?"

"I didn't say that. We're never going to forget about her. But you can't sit in your room half the time or only talk to us when you're not in a bad mood. You can't mope around forever and make stuff up."

"But…," Zack began, and instantly his thoughts were confused. He stepped forward, and as he did, Miriam moved to him and put her arms around his shoulders.

"It's okay, Z," she said. "Really. It's okay. I'm not mad. I'm just trying to let you know…"

Zack began to sob into his sister's embrace, and Miriam held him as the tears continued to come. He felt his sister's hand patting him soothingly on his back, and he drew slowly from her and put a hand to his eyes but kept them closed.

"It's always so nice out here," Miriam said softly. "It's going to be amazing when we open up the Tower again, and everyone can come see it."

"Do you think that story is true, Mir?" Zack said, almost a whisper, with his eyes still closed. "About the Tower making everything around here better?"

She put a hand on his back once again. "I do, Z. I really do."

He opened his eyes and smiled weakly at her.

"Let's get home," she said, and—after a moment—the two of them turned and headed to the house.

The next week passed much as the one before it had, with the work crew continuing to renovate the house and spruce up the property, and the Einsteins steadily progressing on making the mansion into a real home—and a real bed-and-breakfast. A basketball hoop went in at the end of the driveway behind the house, and Miriam occupied hours of each day practicing her shots. Ethan began jogging daily along the main road in preparation for joining his new school's cross-country team. And Ruth discovered there was a weekly writing group at the library in Thornton Falls and began working on some short stories to share with them. The state inspector arrived one day to do an assessment of the Tower (two members of the historical society from Roseburg joined them) and deemed it suitable for use by signing off on a permit. After that, the four kids began scrubbing and polishing and sweeping every surface inside the place over several days; and their parents had a crew come and—within two days—replace all the broken or missing windows.

"It looks almost brand-new," their mother said as the family stood before the Tower on the final day of July and admired it.

"Once we get the roof cleaned up a bit," their father said, "it will look new. It's remarkable how quickly this place shaped up."

Little changed for Zack, either in his routine or his mood: he read (after finishing the tenth Falcons and Bandits book, *Bishop Gee*, he held off on reading the final two books and started in on the Wallenda Quintet series), he stayed in his room much of the time, he joined his siblings on some of their outings to the pools or hiking the trails, and he kept an eye out for Ann. After the strange discussion he'd had with her on the Tower stairs, he had the feeling she wouldn't be coming back for a long time, if at all. Still, the story she had shared had unsettled him badly because it so clearly connected to Horatio's signaling from across the river. Zack resolved to keep all of it to himself for now. Not only did no one in his family believe Ann existed—even he didn't believe that the story she'd told was her own. She had heard it from someone, Zack was positive. That was the only explanation. In addition, Horatio

Cuvallo had become addled, Zack thought, and for whatever reason had begun flashing his odd message across the river as part of his confusion. Maybe one of the people who lived in the cabins had caught sight of the signal and made up a story—Ann had heard it and decided to twist things a bit and share it with Zack. Nothing else made any sense.

At noon on the first day of August, the Einsteins' home was buzzing with activity because the Bigelows were coming for lunch. All four Einstein kids were busy doing something to get the place ready: setting the table, moving all the workers' tools and cords out of the living room and the front corridor, making sure the bathroom was presentable, and looking for the old box of John Coltrane albums their father wanted to play during the meal. The house was also fragrant with their mother's most recent creations: herbed squares of salmon with artichokes, tomatoes, and saffron; a side dish of spicy carrot salad; and a peach pie.

"No way I can compete with Juanita's fried chicken," she announced as the kids watched her take the fish out of the oven, "but I hope they like what I've cooked up."

"Smells good, Mom," Ethan said.

Ruth held up a finger as if to correct him. "It's how it tastes that counts."

Their mother shook her fist at Ruth in mock anger. "You're not

195

eating it anyway, you know. I have lentil soup for all you vegetarians in the house."

"Someday everyone will be a vegetarian," Ruth said. "Trust me. I'm just ahead of the curve."

"Do you know that when you're outside and you're just breathing all regular," Miriam said, "you're inhaling little tiny bugs? Which means you're not a complete vegetarian."

"Here they come!" their father called from the living room. He was looking out the window toward the main road but then turned to address the kids. "I'm counting on everyone to act normal while our guests are here. No discussions about eating bugs or anything like that."

Zack laughed along with the others—the conversation sounded so silly—but he felt slightly agitated. He wanted to know more about Horatio, and he realized his best chance might materialize once the Bigelows were seated at the dining room table.

"Hello, hello!" Rydell said when Morton opened the door and greeted him and Juanita. Within minutes—after Juanita had presented Deborah with a tin of snickerdoodles she'd made and Rydell had commented admiringly on how nicely the renovations inside were coming along—everyone was seated at the table. Morton recited a prayer, and the meal began.

"So you're really going to open up the C.S.—er, the Tower—again?" Juanita said as the conversation wound its way across everything from the weather to what the kids were looking forward to at school to Rydell's mention of a tractor a neighbor up the road had that Morton might be able to get for a good price. "That's such wonderful news."

"We are," Deborah said. "Thanks to the kids. They're the ones who really pushed for it, and I'm glad they did."

"Speaking of the Tower," Morton said, "we have to tell you the strangest thing. It's about that man Horatio. Ethan, why don't you explain—the lights and all that."

Ethan spent the next few minutes sharing details of the flashing lights and the decoding of the message and the visit to Horatio's place, though halfway through his recounting, all the others—aside from Zack—were offering elaboration or correcting one another.

"Well, that is just the oddest thing," Juanita said once the story had been told. She looked at Rydell. "At least we know now where he's been staying."

"That sounds like the old Powter place there across the river," Rydell said. "Those are his cousins. Maybe he took it over or they're letting him stay there. Hard to know what that man's up to, flashing those lights like that."

"But what if he's really trying to communicate with someone?" Zack said.

A moment of silence followed, but Juanita filled it quickly. "How so, dear?" she said.

"What if he thinks someone is lost, and he wants that person to come to him?" Zack said.

"Then I think that would be very generous of him," Juanita said kindly. "He certainly seems unpleasant to the rest of us, but perhaps he's trying to help someone. I like to think that might be the case."

"But why would he try to find someone by flashing lights at the Tower on Saturday nights?" Miriam said. "It just seems so random, like he's just doing it because he's sort of...well, you know, confused or something."

"But what if someone got lost, and he'd worked out a system with that person to help them not be lost?" Zack said, so insistently that everyone at the table stopped eating and looked at him. The moment became fraught and, almost immediately, uncomfortable.

"Zack," his mother said, "it's a very nice idea, and it's kind of you to want to think that way about Mr. Cuvallo. But I think he's probably just flashing those lights because he's a little confused, like Miriam says. I don't believe he's trying to contact any particular person."

Zack stared at his mother. He was about to tell everyone about Ann and the story she'd told him, if only because he felt, once again, it would prove to all of them—so plainly—that everything was coming together somehow, that there was logic and purpose to things.

"Who's that?" Ruth said, looking toward the large window on the far side of the dining room.

Everyone turned to see a car coming up the road. It stopped

just before the house, and a young woman got out and headed for the door.

"That's Megan Rashid, from the post office," Juanita said. "I wonder what she's doing here."

Morton went to open the front door, and everyone heard a brief and muffled conversation; and then Morton returned with a letter that he held up for everyone to see.

"Certified," he said. "I had to sign for it. Special delivery." He examined the return address. "From the county courthouse."

"What's it about?" Ethan said.

His father gestured to the table. "We have a nice lunch here and our wonderful guests. I'll open this later."

"It has to do with Horatio," Miriam said. "I just know it. That's some kind of legal thing."

"Maybe it's good news," Juanita said. "I'm sure you're eager to know what it's about. Please don't hold off on our account."

"You'll be on pins and needles the rest of the time here," Rydell said. "We'll all be trying to enjoy Deborah's pie and my wife's cookies, but you'll be thinking about the little piece of paper inside that envelope. Go ahead and open it. Maybe we can help you make sense of the thing."

Morton looked at Deborah, who gave him a tiny shrug as if to say *Why not?* He ran his eyes over the kids, and then, with a single deft slice of his finger across the top flap, tore open the letter and removed the paper within.

"What's it say?" Ruth asked her father. Everyone was staring at him as he examined the note.

"There's going to be a hearing on September the third," he said, after a moment of reading the paper in silence. "The folks at the county are looking into things, and they'll let us know then what the decision is about moving forward with our bed-and-breakfast. We can provide input during the hearing as part of the process. That's it, basically." He glanced at the letter once more as if to make sure he hadn't left anything out, and then he returned the paper to the envelope and set it on the bureau behind him.

"Well, that sounds like a positive step," Juanita said. "At least it didn't say they've decided you're breaking any laws."

Morton sat glumly. "No, it didn't," he said, though he sounded so flat, everyone looked at him and waited to hear more.

"It's not a disaster," Deborah said. "We have a hearing date, Mort. That's good, I think. Now we know what lies ahead." She put a hand on her husband's arm. "What's wrong?"

"We're supposed to put a halt—immediately—to any more work on the house to make it ready for guests," he said. "That was the last thing in the letter: *All renovations for purposes of establishing a business must cease upon receipt of this note* is what it said." He looked up and sighed.

"We have to stop getting the house fixed up?" Ethan said.

His father nodded. "We can't prepare the place to open. At least not before the hearing."

— Twenty-One —

POSSIBILITIES AND SOLUTIONS

Everyone tried to put on a happy face as lunch concluded and dessert began. But there was no doubt the letter had made the afternoon a bit less cheerful.

"I'd say the glass is half-full," Rydell said while eating a piece of Deborah's peach pie. "There could have been a ruling against you already, and then you'd be looking at a legal fight just to have your day in court. At least this way you can talk it over with the judge, and I'm sure they'll listen to reason."

"Or they'll see an outsider coming here to Vista Point," Morton said gloomily, "and they'll feel the long-standing rights of the community need to be upheld."

"I don't think so," Juanita said. "Besides, once Horatio speaks—if he does—it will be clear this is nothing more than a personal vendetta the man has. He's bitter. That's all. I don't think any ruling will go in his favor."

"I can't understand why he's so angry all the time," Ethan said. You should have seen him. He was really mad."

"We've seen it," Rydell said. "Believe me."

"It's all because of losing the house so many years ago?" Ruth said. "It seems like most people would have gotten over it."

"That and losing his wife and daughter, I imagine," Juanita said. "He could never get past the hurt."

"It really is a shame," Deborah said. "He's such a bitter man. It can't be a good way to lead a life."

"Do you know we were going through our bookshelves last week," Juanita said, "and we found some children's books we'd completely forgotten we had." She looked at the faces staring back at her, and a note of realization came into her eyes. "The reason I mention this is because we found one that must have belonged to Horatio's daughter. Don't ask me how it ended up with us, because I've long since forgotten. Maybe Horatio got rid of the girl's books after she and her mother left, or maybe the girl herself left it at the library and it came into our hands when I worked there. I don't know. I can't remember."

A buzz began to sound in the back of Zack's head, and he sat motionless waiting for Juanita to say more.

"What brings this up, Juanita?" Deborah said.

"Well, it just seemed like such an odd coincidence," she said. "We hadn't thought about the girl in years, and then this happens."

"What book was it?" Zack said. His voice was so soft, Juanita asked him to repeat himself.

"Her book," Zack said. "What was it?"

"I don't know if kids still read it today," she said, "but it's called *Falcons and Bandits*."

"That's Zack's favorite!" Ruth said. "Incredible!"

Ethan lowered his eyebrows and looked at Zack. "That's a pretty strange coincidence," he said, but Zack was too overcome with excitement and confusion to focus on his brother's words.

"How do you know it belonged to her?" Zack said.

"Her name was written in the front," Juanita said. "Felicia Ann Cuvallo. In fact, I think Horatio always called her by her middle name, if I recall correctly."

Zack dropped his fork on the table and lifted both hands before him in something that looked like anguish: This was too much to take in.

"I've seen her," he said, scanning the faces before him. "We've gone exploring in the forest together. I've seen her now, like, five or six times. And she knows all about the lights, too. She told me her father told her to go to the Tower at ten on a Saturday night if she got lost, and he would flash Morse code to her. It's her! I've seen her!" He looked frantically from one face to the next, but everyone simply looked at him without speaking.

"Doesn't anyone believe me?" he said.

"Zack, dear," Juanita said, "that girl left years and years ago. She would be older than your parents now. Horatio's an old man. He's older than we are."

"But I've seen her, Mrs. Bigelow," Zack said. "I swear I have. I'm not making it up. Everything I said is true." He caught his father looking to Rydell. "Dad, I know you think I'm making her up, but I'm not. I've really seen her, and I've talked to her and everything!"

"Son," his father said, "I didn't say you're making her up. It's just, you know, it doesn't really add up to the rest of us, if you step back and look at it. Maybe it's just a coincidence. The girl you met is called Ann, it seems, like the middle name of the girl who put her name in that book. But there's nothing more to it."

Zack bit his lower lip hard; he didn't want to cry, and he didn't want to yell or run off, especially because the Bigelows were at the table.

"May I be excused, please?" he said, and his father nodded. Zack stood and, without a word or a glance at anyone else, headed for the stairs.

"It's just a coincidence," Miriam whispered—though Zack couldn't tell to whom she was speaking. The words weren't intended for him to hear, though.

"It's not a coincidence!" Zack called out, and he ran up the stairs.

Five minutes later, Zack was sitting on his bed with the note he'd written—the one with the medallion letters on it—before him.

I'm going to figure this out, he thought. He was angry and uncertain and, suddenly, full of resolve. The imperative to solve the riddle of the medallion was surging through him like a command: It felt crucial and unavoidable, like being informed he had to make a long hike or swim a long distance, had to set his mind and body to an exhausting task, before he could rest. It seemed that he absolutely had to figure out what the words meant, though he couldn't account for this urgency.

And then an answer came to him: *The charm will make*

everything all right—Ann, Susan, the Tower, Vista Point, our family.
I'm sure of it.

Zack got his notebook and a pen, and although he'd worked through so many possibilities with the medallion lines already, he found himself filling up two whole pages with various combinations of letters in as many different ways as he could. His frustration mounted; he felt he was simply repeating exercises he'd already attempted.

One of Nine, he thought. *The ninth is one.* He could practically hear Ann explaining multiplication tables to him, telling him the clever thing she'd learned about multiplication. He pictured Orland Wetherill's tombstone and the medallion itself. *One of Nine.* He pictured the cabin. *The ninth is one.* The two numbers—nine and one—sounded in his head like a drumbeat; he felt so exasperated by his inability to make any sense of the letters, to make any connection to the numbers one and nine, that he closed his eyes and rubbed his temples to soothe the onset of a headache.

When he opened his eyes and glanced at the clock to see that the time was 5:05, he realized he'd drifted into a long and deep nap. He looked at his notebook beside him as he sat up; something about the number nine had made sense to him in his sleep, he realized, some dream or notion that was slipping away from him as he came fully awake. He tried to hang on to it—he felt desperate to remember what he'd been dreaming.

What if the ninth letter in the final message is the first one in the scrambled lines on the medallion? he thought. *The ninth is one.*

He picked up his pen and began to write on his page without thinking about what he was doing. For nearly twenty minutes, driven by an intuition he couldn't explain, Zack wrote—drawing lines to connect letters, scratching things out, starting over here and there. And when he was done, he was positive he had reached a solution. He read everything over twice, recalculated, counted and marked and checked off—until he finally came to a stop.

He rose from the bed, taking his notebook and pen with him, and he opened his bedroom door to walk downstairs, so filled with excitement, he wanted to shout. When he reached the first floor, Ruth and Ethan were sitting at the dining room table playing backgammon; their mother was making something in the kitchen.

"Zack," Ruth said brightly, looking up when she saw him.

"Hey, Z," Ethan said. He paused, his face shifting quickly from a smile to uncertainty. "You all right?"

Zack took two steps forward. "I figured out what's written on the medallion," he said, holding out his notebook in confirmation. "I know what it says."

Twenty-Two

THE SECRET OF THE MEDALLION

The number nine just kept staying in my head," Zack said when, five minutes later, the other members of the family were seated at the dining room table with him. "I kept thinking there had to be something about that number."

"What do you have, Zack?" his father said. "We can't wait to see what you found."

Zack opened his notebook to show where he'd written, in big letters, the outermost circle of letters: *Fplribsre ielltoana leankedid nttsgntda htotioneo ormudssdo etsepwus.*

"I'm starting with the *F*," Zack said, "because it's capitalized, and that has to be for a reason. I kept thinking that was the first letter of the charm, and I tried all sorts of combinations of substituting letters, like you guys said." He looked to his siblings. "Or shifting letters by nine, or jumping ahead from the *F* by nines and all that stuff. But nothing worked. The thing that seemed weird to me was that there are six groups of nine letters and then one of eight letters at the end, for a total of sixty-two. So I thought, no matter how I rearrange things, the line has to have a total of sixty-two letters. So I made sixty-two blank spots to fill in."

He showed the others at the table what looked like lines in which letters could be entered, just as in hangman—with sixty-two in total:

_ _
_ _
_ _ _ _ _ _

"For some reason," Zack said, "it came to me that maybe the *F* wasn't supposed to be the first letter but the ninth. Like, maybe the letters were all supposed to be counted off in nines. The ninth letter in the final message is taken from the first letter in the mixed-up letters on the medallion."

He added it to the line of spaces he'd created:

_ _ _ _ _ _ _ _ F _ _ _ _ _ _ _ _ _ _ _ _ _ _ _ _ _ _ _
_ _
_ _ _ _ _ _

"And then I thought, what if I just worked ahead by nines after that?" he continued. "So here's how you would do it with the first six letters, by plugging them in every nine spots. You go *f, p, l, r, i, b.* Nine, eighteen, twenty-seven, and keep going. Like this."

```
_ _ _ _ _ _ _ _ F _ _ _ _ _ _ _ _ P _ _ _ _ _ _ _ _ L _
_ _ _ _ _ _ _ R _ _ _ _ _ _ _ _ I _ _ _ _ _ _ _ _ B _ _
_ _ _ _ _ _
```

"And then to keep adding letters, you go back to the beginning of the line of blank spots. Whenever you reach the end of a line, you just keep counting from the start of the line. So for the first bunch of letters, you go back to the start of the line with the *s* and then keep moving ahead every nine spaces to add the *r* and the *e.*"

```
S _ _ _ _ _ _ F R _ _ _ _ _ _ P E _ _ _ _ _ _ _ L _
_ _ _ _ _ _ R _ _ _ _ _ _ _ _ I _ _ _ _ _ _ _ B _ _
_ _ _ _ _ _
```

"The next group of nine letters are *i-e-l-l-t-o-a-n-a,*" Zack said. "If I add those in, starting where I left off after the *e* and counting ahead nine for each letter, you get this."

```
S T _ _ _ _ _ _ F R O _ _ _ _ _ P E A _ _ _ _ _ L I
N _ _ _ _ _ R E A _ _ _ _ _ _ I L _ _ _ _ _ _ B L _
_ _ _ _ _ _
```

"Zack, this is incredible," his mother said, the first comment anyone had made for several minutes as Zack had walked everyone up to this point. "You figured this all out on your own?"

"He's not done yet, Mom," Miriam said. She circled her hands at Zack to encourage him to keep going; her excitement was flaring. "What does it say, Zack? You have to tell us."

"I'll fill in the rest of the letters here for the first line," Zack said, and he quickly filled in the remaining blanks to reveal the following:

S T A N D O U T F R O N T A N D S P E A K T H E S E L I
N E S T O S P R E A D G O O D W I L L I N T R O U B L E
D T I M E S

"And when you separate it out," Zack said, turning the page of his notebook to reveal the line he'd already written there, "it says this: *Stand out front and speak these lines to spread goodwill in troubled times.*"

"That's what the Bigelows told us about the legend," Ruth said. "And what we read, too, about Orland Wetherill. That you say the charm in front of the Tower!"

"Did you figure out the other two lines, Zack?" Ethan said. "Do they follow the same format?"

Zack nodded. "They do. Exactly the same. Everything works by nines." He turned to a new sheet in his notebook, on which was written the medallion's second line: *Ereretihf eohseucui palirsurl olprtauil esnsvaoad aecurprs.*

"There are fifty-three letters in this one, and if you start with the capital *e* and put it in the ninth spot, and then move on to the *r* and put it in the eighteenth spot, and just keep going like how I did the other one, you get this." Zack showed the others the line of letters he'd jotted on a different page in his notebook:

THISPLACEISPUREOURHEARTSAREF
ULLANDPRECIOUSAREOURLIVES

"And when you space them out right," he said, "they spell out *This place is pure, our hearts are full, and precious are our lives.*" He looked up from his notebook to see the faces of the five others staring back at him raptly.

"I figured it out," Zack said.

"The last line, Zack," his mother said. "What's it say? Can you just tell us?"

"I worked it out here," Zack said, turning to the next page, on which was written the third line: *Tssudthpe rshiaseuu snstrsbwm hvwreaeii ipkgvteoe oehfssos.*

"It turns into this." Zack displayed the next page:

THUSWITHTHISBRIEFSPANWEPOSSE
SSMAKESURETHEGOODSURVIVES

"And that turns into *Thus with this brief span we possess, make sure the good survives,*" he said. "The whole thing is *Stand out front and speak these lines to spread goodwill in troubled times. This place is pure, our hearts are full, and precious are our lives. Thus with this brief span we possess, make sure the good survives."*

He looked up. "That's the charm. That's what we need to say in front of the Tower once we get it all fixed up."

"Zack, you're a genius!" Ethan said, throwing his arm around Zack's shoulders.

Their father moved his face closer to the notebook to examine the three-line charm. He pushed his glasses so that they wouldn't slide down his nose, and he studied the words for a long minute before looking up.

"This is spectacular, Zack," he said, his voice full of something that sounded like awe. "How you figured this out. I'm really stunned—and proud of you."

"*Super-spy Zack Einstein began his career as a master code breaker when he was eleven years old,*" Ruth said, and the tension in the room broke as everyone began to laugh.

"Mom and Dad?" Zack said, looking at his parents. "We don't have to stop work on the Tower, do we? It's just the house, right?"

"That's right," his mother said. "Our bed-and-breakfast was the only thing called out in the letter."

"Couldn't we have the work crew spend their time making the last fix-ups on the Tower, then?" Zack said. "And all of us could help finish it up, too."

"I think it's a great idea," his father said, agreeing so rapidly that

Zack wondered if maybe that had been his parents' plan all along.

"Could we open it up when it's done?" Ethan said. "We wouldn't charge anyone to come here."

"And people could show their art, too," Ruth said. "Like Zack suggested."

"Yeah," Ethan continued. "It would be a place where they could look at the view and crafts and stuff, so it wouldn't be like part of our business or anything."

This was Zack's hope exactly. From the moment he'd solved the medallion's message, he'd been thinking that the next step would be to make the Tower as good as new and open it back up for people to enjoy. Once that happened—once it was a place for people to admire and experience—the charm could be spoken before it, and maybe, if the legend was true, some sort of positive feeling would radiate from it, would inspire the people who visited, and make things all right. Maybe Ann would return as well, and whatever bad feelings had arisen between her and Zack would be set aside. If there really was some way that she was the girl Horatio Cuvallo had been searching for and waiting for all these years, then maybe the restoration of the Tower would help them both somehow.

"We've got to open the Tower," Miriam said just as Zack was about to say the same words.

"Why don't we have a big celebration?" Ethan said.

"A jubilee!" Ruth said. "That's what they're called in stories. A jubilee."

Their mother looked to their father. "We could do it, you know. The Tower is getting close to being ready."

"I'm all for it," their father said. "We'll open the Tower."

Ruth had turned to a page in her journal and was examining something. "According to my calendar," she said, "two weeks from this Saturday will be the seventeenth. We could do it then."

"I think we need to give ourselves just a little more time," her mother said.

Ruth glanced back at her journal. "The Saturday after that would be the…" She stopped speaking and looked up, her expression suddenly somber, as though she'd made some awful mistake and wanted to take back her words.

"The twenty-fourth," Miriam said softly, looking just as subdued as Ruth had become.

"One year exactly since Susan…," Ethan began, and the six members of the family cast glances at one another as the realization sank in.

Their mother shifted her eyes quickly across the others and then said, "I think we should aim for the twenty-fourth. Jubilee at Vista Point, August twenty-fourth."

"Deb," their father said, his tone cautious and uncertain. "I think we should choose a different—"

She began speaking before he'd concluded his sentence. "It will be good for all of us. A way to honor Susan, when you think about it. Like a gift not only to everyone here in the area but also to her. A commemoration."

Ethan looked at Zack and then at their mother. "That would be kind of nice," he said. "That way it makes the day kind of like something really positive, I think."

"It feels like we would be celebrating on that day, though," Miriam said. "It seems a little weird to me." She pulled her lips in and appeared to be considering things; and then she turned to Zack.

"What do you think, Z?" she said.

Zack was well aware that the calendar had nearly circled back to that awful night from the year before, though he'd lost track of just how quickly the date was drawing near. He wasn't sure what he thought about holding the jubilee on the one-year anniversary, though as he allowed Miriam's question to sink in, the notion of saying the charm on the very day itself seemed to make absolute sense. There was a soundness to it that made him feel everything would turn out right, that things would fall into place, that some order would be restored. Susan, Ann, the charm, maybe even Horatio Cuvallo somehow—if Orland Wetherill's legend had any shred of validity to it, then maybe August 24 was the right day to open the Tower.

"I think that sounds perfect," he said.

His father nodded once with finality. "August twenty-fourth it is," he said. "The Jubilee at Vista Point."

— *Twenty-Three* —

PREPARING FOR A CELEBRATION

Two weeks and four days passed; another Monday arrived. Saturday the twenty-fourth was only a few days away, and the Einsteins were in a final-dash frenzy to make sure the Tower—and their property—was ready for the big jubilee, though everyone felt the celebration was arriving much more quickly than they'd bargained for. An uncharacteristic rainstorm the week before had halted the renovation work on the Tower's roof, the electrical wiring inside was proving tricky to fix, and a problem with the building's plumbing threatened to leave it without water for the bathrooms and drinking fountains.

"Keep your fingers crossed, everyone," their father said as the countdown—five days remaining—began in earnest. "The workers tell me everything's going to be fixed by Saturday, and I'm going to believe them. For now."

The four kids spent hours each day sprucing up the outside of the Tower, clearing the weeded-over parking area and repainting the lines on the road—which had been professionally cleared and cleaned the day after the rain let up—and in the parking lot itself. They also worked on the decorations and signs for the jubilee— ribbons and balloons and streamers for the inside of the Tower, plus signs indicating everything from COOKIES RIGHT HERE! to QUESTIONS? ASK ONE OF US WEARING A BLUE SHIRT!

One of their primary tasks was the delivery of invitations to the jubilee to their neighbors up and down the road, something they accomplished on long days of walking or, when the distance grew too great, by driving with their mother, who dropped them off at the ends of driveways to hand-deliver the invitations wherever they could. Ruth had the idea to invite the people who lived in the cabins in the woods, and on one of the kids' treks through the forest, they visited the group and handed an invitation to the woman who'd been singing while holding her baby weeks before. For everyone, all six of the Einsteins, the days were long and full of work, but no one complained, because it was all in service of a single goal—and because it took everyone's mind off the looming court hearing in September.

Zack was just as engaged as his brother and sisters in the work at hand, no longer feeling the need to retreat to his room or pull away from the others. He joined in on the chores just as every-one else did, right after breakfast each day until nearly dark. The four kids occasionally took breaks to go for a quick swim or to shoot some baskets; but the days were mostly devoted to getting the Tower ready and making sure the house was comfortable—not quite bed-and-breakfast-ready, but nice enough for a family of six. Zack was glad to have the distraction of so much activity because it kept him from contemplating too many things too deeply.

Ann had not reappeared since the morning Zack had seen her on the stairs of the Tower, and although he looked for her often—from his window, in the woods, when he walked in the field on his way to the Tower—she was nowhere to be found. Zack visited the cave every other day, too, and even left notes for her; but there was no indication Ann ever saw them, and, even if she had, she didn't leave any message for Zack in return. Not that any of this surprised him. There had been something very final about her departure the last time they'd been together, something that suggested to Zack she had been hurt by his words and had no intention of seek-ing him out again. Which left him feeling resigned to the notion that perhaps the jubilee would be his next—and maybe his last—opportunity to see her. Because he felt certain she would appear. She *had* to, he thought. It might be his final chance to help her, he believed, to bring to a close whatever she was hoping to discover or solve.

What if she really is lost? he thought, even though this didn't make complete sense to him. Still, he hoped she would appear on the twenty-fourth. *I can help her* was the notion he consoled himself with whenever he felt discouraged by the thought that she had no desire to see him.

On the Monday before the jubilee, the Einsteins had taken a break for lunch when the mail deliverer, Megan Rashid, pulled up outside the house just as she had nearly three weeks before, when she'd brought the letter informing their parents of the hearing. This time, their mother went to answer the door and returned a moment later with an envelope that looked just like the one from the previous time. She had a puzzled look on her face.

"Maybe they called the whole thing off!" Ethan said as his mother sat at the table and displayed the envelope as if it were some exotic little packet that had dropped from the sky and ended up in their yard. She seemed to be assessing not only what it might be but whether it was even intended for her and Morton.

"If they did call it off," Morton said, "that would be very welcome news." He bobbed his head toward the envelope. "Can you do the honors, Deb?" he said, and she opened the letter.

"What's it say, Mom?" Miriam asked. The look on their mother's face was inscrutable. "Is it good or bad?"

Their mother looked up. "Well, neither, really. I'm not sure." She handed the letter to her husband as she said, "They want to hold the hearing a little earlier than they'd planned, which is actually something we asked them to consider. We wanted it sooner rather than later, so we wouldn't be held up for so long on getting the place ready. And it looks like they're going to grant our request."

Their father was studying the letter himself, and his expression became just as hard to read as their mother's. He pressed his face closer to the page as if to make sense of something on it.

"You mean we won't have to wait until September for the hearing?" Ethan said. His mother nodded; his father was completely absorbed in studying the letter, though in the silence that was gathering, he slowly raised his head.

"So, when is it?" Ruth said.

As if they'd planned it, their parents answered at the same time: "This Friday."

"The day before the jubilee?" Zack said.

"Looks like it," his mother said.

"That's—that's—" Miriam sputtered. "That's impossible! With everything we're trying to do to get ready, the hearing is going to be right before our celebration?"

"Of all the days," Ethan said.

Their mother took the letter back from their father and set it on the table. "Let's hope for a good outcome on Friday. The jubilee will either be a lot of fun and the first day of getting back on track with the bed-and-breakfast…"

"Or," their father said, taking up the thread, "an opportunity for us all to put on our best smiling faces despite bad news. We might be hosting the first *and* last event at our place on Saturday."

Over the next few days, Zack was tempted—as he had been ever since he'd deciphered the medallion's message—to visit the Tower, stand before it, and speak the words aloud. He was nearly certain this would make everything right; but he was a bit more certain he needed to wait until the jubilee, when the Tower was officially reopened. He kept picturing the big day in his thoughts—the throng of guests, the decorations everywhere, the tables of food. His mother and Ethan, mainly, had been busy making cookies and deviled eggs and trays of vegetables and fruit—even a few loaves of challah, something they all enjoyed during their Friday night dinners. Ruth and Miriam had perfected a lime punch, and they were also in charge of arranging platters of crackers and cheese. There was going to be a three-man band, too (Rydell on clarinet, with two of his friends playing trumpet and drums); and their mother and father had worked up a speech but hadn't yet shared it with the kids. Finally, starting it all off before the guests arrived, the Einsteins would—as they'd discussed several times now—arrange themselves on the stairs of the Tower and say the charm. Once spoken, Zack believed, the day couldn't help but be a success. And so he told himself the charm had to wait until Saturday.

The most immediate matter, though, aside from the exhausting labor of finalizing so many things in preparation, was the hearing. Their parents had been fretting over it since they'd received the initial notice, of course; but they and the kids had deferred giving it too much thought while preparing for the jubilee. Now all that had been upended, and a focus on the hearing had to take priority for their parents while the kids continued their work and anxiously looked to Friday.

"The day will arrive," their father said on Wednesday. "Your mother and I will say what we need to say, and then we'll leave it up to the judge to decide."

Their mother shrugged. "There's nothing more we can do."

And then Friday came. Half an hour before noon, as the kids sat in the living room making plans for the tasks they were going to complete over the final hours leading up to the jubilee (cookie baking for Ethan, hanging streamers in the Tower for Miriam and Zack, writing out the last fifty *Welcome to the Vista Point Jubilee!* cards for Ruth), their parents came downstairs.

"Well, we're off," their father said. He was wearing an ill-fitting brown suit, something that the kids saw him put on only for the occasional wedding or bar mitzvah and that made him appear deeply uncomfortable. The look on his face, something sour and tired, didn't help.

"Don't feel like you guys have to finish everything," their mother said. She looked uncommonly composed, even though she, too, was wearing clothing—a blue dress and a cashmere vest—that was very uncharacteristic. "We hope to be home by dinnertime at the latest, but we're at the mercy of how things get scheduled."

"We have to show up by one o'clock," their father said.

The four kids rose and, one by one, offered their parents hugs.

"Good luck," Ruth said.

"I know the judge is going to say everything's okay," Miriam said.

"We have it all covered here," Ethan said. "Don't worry."

Zack stepped forward. "Mom?" he said. "Dad?"

Everyone was staring at Zack, uncertain what was about to come out of his mouth.

"You," he said. "Great parents. How to win in front of the judge and all the other people at the courthouse."

A stunned silence followed—and Zack, who hadn't been completely convinced himself that he would deliver this little joke he'd planned, wondered if maybe he'd said the wrong thing—and then everyone broke into laughter and patted Zack on the shoulders, and Ethan put him in a playful headlock.

"You got us with that one, Zack!" his father said. "I wasn't expecting that."

Zack looked at his mother and father, beaming. "Really what I wanted to say was I hope it goes well." He paused. "And I love you."

— *Twenty-Four* —

THE JUBILEE AT VISTA POINT

Their parents hadn't returned by six o'clock that evening, and the kids were getting worried. But when the car finally pulled up and their parents opened the door and came inside, it was impossible for the kids to read their faces.

"Well?" Ethan said. "What happened?"

"Yeah," Miriam said. "You were gone so long."

"Quite a day," their father said, running a hand through his hair.

"And?" Ruth said. "What was the decision?"

"That's the thing," their mother said, plopping down on the couch to remove her shoes. "We don't know. They didn't make a ruling yet. We thought they were going to."

"We *hoped* they were going to," their father said, "but I guess we didn't completely realize this was just a way for the judge to get information. Then he'll make a ruling."

"Wait, there's no decision yet?" Miriam said. "Nothing at all?"

"Nothing at all," their mother said.

"Well, that doesn't seem fair," Ethan said. "You two went through all of that, and we spent the whole week worrying, and now we won't even know the outcome for…who knows when?"

Their mother sat back heavily on the couch and sighed. "It's just the way it is, Ethan. At least the hard part is over. We spoke, the judge listened. Now all we can do is wait."

Their father stood and set his suit jacket on the closest chair. "And get back to work. I'm going to go change, and then we should light the Shabbat candles for prayers, and if no one's had dinner, we can have a quick bite. After that"—he snapped his fingers—"we should get crackin'."

The kids stared at him, dumbfounded; it seemed he'd switched gears in an instant, and they were surprised—and encouraged—by his display of enthusiasm.

"Because you know, everyone," he said, "we have a jubilee to throw tomorrow."

Morning arrived. The celebration was slated to begin at one o'clock, and so at noon exactly—once the food was ready, and the decorations and everything else were in place, and it seemed the Einsteins could do nothing more to prepare for the gathering—the six members of the family had a quick lunch, put on their blue *Vista Point Jubilee 2002!* T-shirts, and made a steady, resolute walk across the field to the Tower. The August day was bright and warm, with a cloudless sky and no wind; from far off, a perfume of blackberries ripening in the late-summer warmth drifted to them, mingling with the smell of the dry grass all around. The familiar and nearly indistinguishable buzz sounded in Zack's ears as he walked, though he never had determined whether it was the sound of the river below or the accumulated beat of the distant waterfalls in all directions or the humming of insects or even just the swish of the air in his ears—but the low vibration was reassuring and calming, and as he walked with the others, the Tower looming before them, he focused on the sound.

No one spoke; a feeling of reverence, of something special about to unfold, held the six of them as they approached the edge of the bluff just beside the stone building, its windows clear and gleaming and its new bronze-colored cap glistening in the sunlight. They walked around to the front of the Tower, the river appearing below them in a brilliant ribbon of blue. Zack scanned the forest on the far side of the water and wondered if Horatio was over there somewhere, maybe getting ready to drive across to Vista Point, maybe thinking of Ann or the Einsteins and the opportunity the day held.

Everyone stopped before the stairs and looked around; it was as if something was about to happen, as if there was someone to meet.

Their father held a hand out to their mother. "Won't you join me, Deb?" he said, and the two of them ascended the stairs.

"Come on, everyone," he added, and the kids followed.

The six of them stood just before the Tower's doors, the sunlight directly on them. They all looked to one another with some combination of awe and uncertainty and sympathy, as though they didn't know what might come next but they were glad to be with one another.

"Seven Einsteins," their mother said suddenly, her voice so resolute and her words so unexpected, Zack gave a start. "Morton, Deborah, Ethan, Miriam, Ruth, Zack, and Susan. Seven of us together, always, no matter what."

"One of us was lost a year ago," their father said. "At least, that part of her we could see and hear and touch. But she wasn't lost in the most important way." He put a hand on his chest. "In here, where we hold her memory and keep her love alive within us. In that sense, she will never be lost."

"It's been one year exactly," their mother said. "And I believe that today, here, now, Susan has somehow found her way to us, that she's here with us." She held her hands out, one to her husband and one to Ethan beside her; and then everyone was holding hands, their eyes closed, their heads bowed. "She will never be lost. And we'll never be lost as long as we have each other."

Silence held for a moment, and then their father said, "Zack, you figured out the charm. Can you say it for us now?"

A ripple of something like apprehension and hope and sadness and excitement all mixed together ran through Zack, something stronger than any of the strange and confusing feelings that had been consuming him for twelve months. He kept his eyes closed and heard the buzzing in his head anew, and an image of Susan came to him, of her smiling at him, of her gazing simply and sincerely at him.

A slight breeze began to blow.

"This place is pure," Zack recited, the words coming softly but with absolute assurance, "our hearts are full, and precious are our lives." He paused momentarily and gripped Miriam's and his mom's hands more firmly before continuing. He felt the gentle wind on his face. "Thus with this brief span we possess," he said, "make sure the good survives."

Utter silence surrounded the family.

"Make sure the good survives," Miriam said.

"Make sure the good survives," echoed Ruth, and then Ethan, and their parents said the same words in turn, and everyone opened their eyes—hands still clasped—and looked about.

"I felt something," Ruth said after a moment.

"So did I," Ethan said. "Like a little wind on my face."

"Me too," Miriam said. "Right as we said the words. I felt something."

She looked to Zack—they all did—and he nodded quickly. "I felt the same thing," he said. "I think she…," he began. "I think Susan…," he tried again. He squeezed his sisters' hands. "I felt something for sure."

Their parents exchanged a glance with each other. They looked somewhere between amazed and delighted, and it was clear to Zack that they, too, had felt whatever it was the others had felt—a presence, a sign, an indication of something that none of them could define but that each one of them had understood in their heart.

It was several moments before everyone let go of the hands they were holding. And then their father plucked at his T-shirt, gave a gentle smile, and said, "It's time for the Vista Point Jubilee. I think we're ready to begin."

To everyone's surprise, their mother jumped down the stairs and began trotting off. "Back to the house," she called. "Let's get the food out here and get ready. The guests are on their way!"

"Mom's running?" Miriam said, squinting at their mother as though watching her perform some strange dance.

"That she is," their father said, and he skipped down the steps. "And I'm joining her! Come on!"

By one thirty, the parking area just southwest of the Tower was three-quarters full; at least a hundred and fifty people were wandering inside the stone building or admiring the views from the bluff or enjoying the refreshments arranged on the tables just beside the Tower; and Rydell's three-man band was starting to play. Ruth sat just inside the doors of the Tower, where she greeted visitors and invited them to sign the big white guest book she'd prepared. Miriam held two red flags and was guiding the cars that arrived at the parking area. Ethan was on the outside stairs of the Tower beside a stand that read ASK ME ABOUT THE HISTORY AND GEOGRAPHY OF THE AREA, where he was detailing the background of the building for a group of fifteen listeners. Deborah and Morton stood beside a lectern set up at the base of the outside stairs, and they greeted everyone who arrived—neighbors they'd already met and some they were just meeting for the first time. And Zack helped Juanita keep the tables stocked with food and punch, the latter going quickly because the day was warming up quite a bit. As he went about his errands, though, Zack kept an eye out at all times for Ann, though he saw only the scores of people who'd come simply to admire the Tower

and honor its reopening. He looked for Horatio, too, but there was no sign of him. Zack recognized one of the men from the camp in the woods among the crowd, and with him was the woman who'd been singing; she had her baby with her, and a few other people accompanied them, all of them mingling easily with the rest of the crowd.

At two fifteen, after Rydell's band had livened up the attendees with several fast numbers, Morton stepped up to the lectern and used his booming voice to get everyone's attention.

"Can folks take a seat, please?" he called, indicating the nine rows of folding chairs arranged before him. "And if there's not a seat, I'll invite you to stand in the back there." He turned to the door of the Tower. "Ruth, can you ask the people inside to come out? Thanks."

It took a few minutes, but before long, a throng of nearly two hundred people were standing or sitting before Morton and Deborah, who were at the lectern at the base of the stairs, with the Tower behind them; and everyone was ready to hear what the two of them would say.

"Good afternoon," Deborah said with a little wave. "My goodness, we didn't expect so many people, but we're very glad you're all here. Welcome to the Vista Point Jubilee—which we hope will be the first of many of these annual events to come—and welcome to the reopening of the Vista Point Comfort Station—or, as we like to call it, the Tower!" She gestured to the building behind her, and everyone applauded. Zack had moved to one side of the crowd, where he could see his parents easily and admire the Tower in front of which they stood.

"We'd like to thank several people who made this day possible," Deborah said, and she moved into offering appreciation to the workers, some of the people in the area who'd provided assistance, and the kids themselves. And then Morton took over and began to detail some of the history of the Tower, and the renovation work that had been done, and how—with the blessing of the historical society—the Einsteins would be taking over the upkeep and perhaps even the ownership of the Tower. The audience listened attentively; Zack kept scanning all around, even the woods, but no one new had appeared.

"I can't say this whole endeavor has proceeded without some difficulties," his father said. "I guess that's to be expected, but we hope to have everything smoothed out very soon. One thing we learned as we embarked on this plan to fix up the place and set down roots here was that the Tower used to be a place where people came to gather and enjoy themselves. My wife and I and our kids—really, our kids mostly, and of the four of them, our eleven-year-old, Zack, most of all—had an idea that maybe we could establish the Tower as a place for local artists and craftspeople to display their work. Maybe even sell their work, if we figure out how to go about making sure that's okay. Anyway, if there's any of you out in the audience who think this is a good idea and want to help with the effort, please come talk to us afterward."

Several calls of assent rose from the crowd as everyone began to applaud; Deborah looked approvingly at Morton, though the moment was interrupted by the sound of a vehicle skidding loudly as it entered from the main road and, it seemed, taking the first bend toward the Tower too quickly. Everyone turned to look. A pickup truck approached the parking lot, the noise of its loud engine cutting through the afternoon heat. His father resumed talking, but Zack kept his eyes on the truck. It pulled into a parking spot, and from it stepped Horatio Cuvallo, dressed in his corduroy pants and flannel shirt once again, as though the month wasn't August but maybe something closer to Thanksgiving.

Zack spotted Ruth standing at the far end of the row opposite him, and she flashed him a look that seemed to say *Let's hope there isn't any trouble now*, which was exactly what Zack was thinking.

"And we plan to keep the Tower open," their father was saying, "so that visitors and sightseers can come here and enjoy the view. That's something we will be proud to do as part of being neighbors and friends to one and all here in…" He stumbled over his words, and Zack understood why: His father's eyes had just landed on Horatio, who'd stalked up to the fringe of the audience and, standing deliberately and very obviously a few feet away from anyone else, had his hands on his hips and was staring defiantly in Morton's direction.

"That is," Morton said, "we're looking forward to being friends to one and all here in Vista Point."

"Our new home," Deborah added, and the applause resumed.

From the center of the crowd, a tiny white-haired woman wearing an elegant red pantsuit stood and raised her hand.

"May I offer a comment, please?" she said.

"Mrs. Ollennu," Deborah said. "Very nice to see you."

"Yes, I'm Ami Ollennu," the woman said, glancing around and offering a small wave in greeting. She had a friendly smile, and it seemed to Zack that many in the audience knew who she was. "The county clerk," she said. "And it's a real pleasure to see so many familiar faces here on this wonderful day."

"We're glad you're here," Morton said. "Please, what would you like to say? Do you have a question?"

"Not a question," she said, her voice lowering, almost quizzical. "More a comment, or rather, a contribution to the proceedings." She turned to her left and then her right, scanning the audience. "Mr. and Mrs. Einstein came to the courthouse for a hearing yesterday because there exists a statute we needed to examine regarding the legality of opening their home as a bed-and-breakfast—as a commercial venture, to put it bluntly. The hearing went until late in the afternoon yesterday, and we were going to defer a decision on it until next week. But after the Einsteins left, Judge Walsh reviewed the details and came to a decision on the matter. He asked me to share that today with the Einsteins." She looked at Morton and Deborah. "I was going to talk to both of you after things had concluded, but it seems there's no time like the present."

She reached into the front pocket of her red jacket, drew out a piece of paper, and unfolded it; and then she reached into the pocket of her white shirt and removed her reading glasses and affixed them to her face slowly and deliberately. Zack was riveted with expectation, and the woman's unhurried preparations felt like torture. But finally she cleared her throat, focused on the page before her, and lifted her chin to speak.

"This is the official statement of the judge," she said. She cleared her throat again and read, in a louder voice, "*The court places no restrictions on the bed-and-breakfast venture as proposed by Morton and Deborah Einstein at the address listed in the appendix of this document, and they are at liberty to proceed with their operation without delay and with no restrictions, according to all appropriate zoning statutes and regulations.*" She looked up. "That's the entirety of the statement."

"We can go ahead with our plans?" Morton said, his eyes wide as he looked at Mrs. Ollennu.

"Yes, you can," she said—and at that, the crowd burst into a riot of cheers and applause and whistles, and Zack turned to the person closest to him—a man who appeared to be nearly eighty years old but with the thickest head of white hair Zack had ever seen—and gave him a high five. Morton and Deborah were hugging, and suddenly Miriam was behind Zack and grabbing him in a hug, too.

"The charm, Z!" she yelled. "It was the charm! It must have worked."

Everyone, it seemed, was smiling or clapping or simply beaming appreciatively at the Tower or at Zack's parents or, perhaps, at the generally festive and happy mood of the day. And Zack felt that Miriam was exactly right: The charm had succeeded. The aura of goodness that radiated from the Tower and suffused the crowd felt absolute and undeniable.

Zack looked all around, thinking that if Ann was going to appear, right now was the moment. His eyes landed on Horatio Cuvallo, whose face was lowered in anger and who was standing where he'd been all along, but now looking as though he wanted to burst with indignation. And it registered with Zack that maybe the power of the charm had not been absolute, that it had extended to nearly everyone at the Tower—but not all.

"Just one minute!" Horatio yelled, his voice booming so loudly that it caused everyone to pause. The light conversation and easy laughter that had arisen in the wake of Ami Ollennu's announcement ceased abruptly, and the eyes of the entire audience were locked on Horatio, who stood defiantly in place and was staring at Morton and Deborah.

"Mr. Cuvallo," Morton said, his voice filling the suddenly jarring silence. "We're glad you joined us today. Would you like to make a comment?"

Zack watched as Horatio leveled an accusing finger at his mother and father, and he felt certain something bad was about to happen.

"You bet I'd like to make a comment," Horatio said. "This is wrong! You have no business setting up shop here. This whole place was stolen from me decades ago, and at the very least you should step back from making money off what used to be my house."

"Leave them be, Horatio!" someone called from the crowd, and Horatio flinched as he looked for whoever had spoken.

"I won't let them be," he said. "The law might have come down on their side, but I'm talking about what's proper. What's just. They stroll in here and take over. It's not right."

"Now's not the time," someone said, and Zack found the source of the voice and saw it was Juanita Bigelow. "We're all gathered here to celebrate the day."

"Where my life was torn apart?" Horatio said. "Here? Does anyone think that's…"

His voice gave out. Zack was staring at him and thought perhaps his anger had gotten the better of him. It seemed he couldn't get any more words to come—but, stranger still, his entire expression had altered, his entire posture. Whereas a moment before he'd appeared to be consumed by rage, he suddenly looked like someone who'd been stunned; his mouth dropped open, and his shoulders slumped.

Zack turned to look at where Horatio was gazing. In front of the doors of the Tower—and just behind his parents—Ann stood smiling. Zack had no presence of mind to consider how she'd ended up there, in the most conspicuous spot and in view of the entire crowd; all he focused on was how completely calm she appeared, as though it was the most natural thing in the world for her to be standing there.

"Ann?" Zack said, the word escaping from him before he could stop himself.

She waved to him, the smile on her face widening. And then she turned to look at Horatio and lifted her hand even higher as she waved more urgently.

Zack turned to look at Horatio, who stood staring in absolute shock.

"Are you okay, Horatio?" Rydell called.

But Horatio said nothing to him—indeed, appeared not to have heard him speak. Instead, he raised his arm to point once again—not accusingly this time, but almost as a reflex—directly at Ann.

"My daughter!" he called.

He rushed toward the stairs of the Tower as Ann slipped inside the stone building.

Twenty-Five

THE SECRET AND THE CHARM

For a moment, Zack thought Horatio was going to knock his father over in his dash toward the doors. But Horatio moved past his parents as though they weren't any concern of his and instead entered the Tower. Zack followed, slowly for a few steps as he moved past the rows of seats, and then quickly, leaping up the stairs.

"Zack, stop!" his father said. He looked to the half-opened Tower doors in complete bafflement; it seemed he could make no sense of what had just happened.

"It's Ann," Zack said. "The girl I told you about. My friend."

"What do you mean, Zack?" his mother said. "What's going on?"

But right then, Zack, too, entered the Tower and found Ann and Horatio standing before each other in the delicate light, both looking as though they could not understand what they were seeing.

"Is it you?" Horatio said to her, almost whispering.

Ann nodded. "It is. I came back." She pointed to Zack. "He helped me."

Horatio turned to Zack without seeming to understand what Ann meant.

"We met here," Zack said. "In the Tower."

"But how?" Horatio said. "How are you here, Ann?"

She merely smiled gently and then reached a hand out to him. "I wanted to let you know I'm all right, Father."

"*Father*?" Zack said, the word making him feel dizzy.

"Yes," Ann said. "My father."

"I don't understand," Zack said, and then a shadow appeared in the doorway, and Zack turned to see his father.

"Zack, is everything all right?" he said.

"It's okay, Dad," Zack said softly.

"I think you should…," his father said.

Horatio turned to him, his eyes brimming with tears. "My daughter," he said to Morton. "My daughter."

But Morton merely shook his head in incomprehension as he took a step forward. "I don't understand what you're saying, but if you…"

Horatio looked away from him and moved forward to Ann; he knelt and embraced her tightly, the tears flowing freely. "Ann, Ann, Ann," he said. "I never thought I'd see you again."

Morton moved silently to Zack and put a hand on his shoulder. "What is going on?" he whispered, leaning into his son. "Who is he talking to?"

And at that moment Zack understood—maybe not all of it, but the essentials. He watched the two of them, Ann and her father, holding each other as though there was no other moment in life behind them or ahead—there was simply this time, this instant, where whatever sadness had preceded and whatever uncertainty lay ahead was all set aside, all inconsequential when placed beside this moment just now.

"I never thought I'd see you again," Horatio said as he knelt holding his daughter, and Ann simply held him in return as they both pressed their eyes closed, blocking out anything and everything else.

Zack felt the gentle touch of a hand on his shoulder; and when he looked up, his father gave a small gesture with his head toward the door. The two of them moved away. Zack glanced back one final time, but Ann and Horatio hadn't shifted at all—they held each other, and Zack and his father stepped back into the sunlight and left them alone.

Outside, the crowd had resumed talking and getting refreshments or admiring the views on the edge of the bluff; Rydell's band began to play. Whatever Deborah had said after Horatio and Ann and Zack—and Morton—had entered the Tower, it was clear she'd let everyone know the speechmaking had concluded and the leisurely visiting could continue. Before Zack knew it, Ethan, Miriam, and Ruth were on the stairs with him and their father and mother, and everyone was looking at Zack with perplexity.

"What's happening in there?" Miriam said. "What did he mean when he said something about his daughter?"

Zack simply stared at her; he had no idea how to begin, but just as the words were coming to him, his father spoke.

"Something really powerful and really hard to believe is going on in there right now," their father said. "I can't account for it.

Zack might have some inkling of things, but it might be tough for him to explain it."

"I really did see her," Zack said. "Ann. The girl I told you guys about." He looked behind him at the Tower doors, which his father had closed. "Horatio's her father. I don't understand how she's a little girl and he's an old man, but that's her father. He was in the war years ago, and—I don't know how to explain the whole thing. She told me her father wanted her to come to the Tower if she ever got lost. He would flash lights at her to send her a message."

"The Morse code?" Ethan said. "You mean Horatio was trying to signal to his daughter?"

"But how would she know to look for it?" Miriam said.

"And how would he know she would be there?" Ruth said. "And how can he even be her father if she's as young as you told us?"

Their parents looked at each other, and their mother said, "Didn't the Bigelows say Horatio's daughter left years ago?"

Zack shook his head in confusion. "I don't know how it fits together, really. I don't understand the whole thing, but…"

The Tower doors opened, and Horatio stepped out. He seemed dazed, as though he'd just walked away from some accident or disaster and couldn't believe he was still in one piece; but he had a soft look on his face that made him appear transformed, like a different person from the one the Einsteins had encountered before. All the anger had drained away.

"Mr. Cuvallo," Deborah said, "are you okay?"

Horatio looked to Zack, and, as if guessing what was on his mind, said, "She says goodbye. She wanted me to tell you that."

"Goodbye?" Zack said. He pointed behind Horatio. "Isn't she in there?"

"She was," Horatio said. "We talked for just a couple of minutes, and then she told me she had to leave. I hugged her again, and then she wasn't there."

Zack felt a surge of alarm go through him, and he took two steps closer to the doors and peered inside. The Tower was empty—even on the stairs leading up to the second level and on the balcony that rimmed it, no one was visible.

Morton gestured to the chair just inside the Tower doors, where Ruth had been sitting with the guest book. "Would you like to sit down?" he said to Horatio, who, in answer, turned, went inside, and dropped heavily into the seat. The Einsteins followed him; their father pulled the door closed behind them, and everyone looked at Horatio as he began to speak.

"Ann and her mother—my ex-wife, Janet—left me back in sixty-six," he said.

"You don't have to go into any of it right now, Mr. Cuvallo," Deborah said. "Really. It's okay."

Horatio closed his eyes momentarily and lifted a hand as if to say he wanted to continue. "It was my fault that she left," he said. "If I'm honest about it. They moved way down south, and we lost track of each other pretty quickly. And then I joined the army to try to forget everything. Vietnam. It's a long story, but they had me listed as missing in action, and I guess that report somehow filtered back to my ex-wife. She thought I was dead, and when I finally came back to the States, I decided it was probably best to leave it like that and not bother her—or Ann—with my problems. Ann told me, just now, she thought I died years ago. They both did. She told me she and her mother led a good life, and I'm glad to know that finally. It was always a mystery to me, something I didn't want to look into."

He put a hand to his forehead and closed his eyes. "I wasted so many years. I guess I can say that now."

The Tower became silent as everyone waited for Horatio to continue.

"I don't understand, though," Zack said. "If Ann was your daughter and she moved away a long time ago…"

"She passed away," Horatio said, opening his eyes and looking to Zack.

"Passed away?" Zack said weakly. "But I've seen her a bunch of times. At the Tower and in the woods. She even took me to the cave that you showed her."

Horatio's eyes lit up, and he nearly smiled. "She showed that to you?"

"And the old stump nearby," Zack said. "And she told me about how you told her to come to the Tower if she got lost." He glanced at his siblings and his parents. "She didn't pass away. I saw her, and we talked about all kinds of things."

Horatio nodded slowly. "She just explained it all to me. She passed away a little over two months ago. Which is right when I started to get the feeling I needed to begin flashing those lights, just like I told her years ago that I would. I didn't know why the need to do so came over me, but it makes sense now." He put a hand to his forehead again and paused. "She died of cancer in the middle of June. She was forty-five, and her dying wish was to comfort me. To come back the way I remembered her and find me again. And she did. It wasn't until just now that she remembered who she really was and what happened to her. Until a few moments ago inside there, she thought she was a nine-year-old girl. My little girl."

"Do you mean," Miriam said, "she was...she was a..." She looked to Ruth.

"Her spirit came back here," Ruth said softly.

Ethan looked to Zack. "And you saw her, too? You really did?"

Zack nodded. Horatio reached out a hand to him—and Zack's first reaction was to draw back, until he saw that the man meant him no harm. He took Horatio's hand.

"I want to thank you," Horatio said. "She told me you were kind to her. She told me she thought there was something about you that allowed her to visit this place where I always told her to come. She said you were looking for someone who was lost, and that was what let her come here."

"Susan," Morton said. "Zack's sister. Our youngest child."

"She passed away one year ago," Deborah said. "Today. This very day."

"I never knew what happened to my daughter," Horatio said, "but she thought I was gone. Now she's gone, but I had one last chance to see her, and I'm going to be grateful for that forever." He looked to Zack. "Thank you. And I owe an apology to all of you for the way I acted, for the way I've been acting for years."

"No need to apologize, Mr. Cuvallo," Morton said. "You've been through a lot. We're just glad you're here with us today."

"And we hope you'll come back again," Deborah said.

Horatio smiled weakly. "I'm glad the ruling went in your favor. I suppose it means you'll be here for a long time now. And that sounds like a good thing to me all of a sudden. I saw my girl one last time, and that means everything to me. I just wish Jing was here to see it, too. Janet, I mean."

The hair stood up on the back of Zack's neck. "Did you say Jing?"

"That was my nickname for my wife. Jing instead of Janet. And she called me Ray instead of Horatio."

"Mr. Cuvallo," Zack said, the words coming haltingly, "I saw your message in the cave. *Always yours*, you wrote."

"What are you talking about, Zack?" his father said, but Horatio was staring at Zack and, once again, looked entirely shaken.

"You saw that?" he said to Zack, who began nodding quickly.

"There's a cave," Zack said, looking to his siblings. "Just down the hill a little bit. Ann showed it to me, and we went there a few times. Mr. Cuvallo carved something on the inside of it a long time ago."

"I did," Horatio said. "For my wife."

"And she wrote something to you," Zack said.

Horatio shook his head in confusion. "No, I just carved that message there once after she left me," he said. "Before I enlisted. One of those times when I went to the cave and was feeling sorry for myself."

"No, she answered you," Zack said. "She must have come back and seen what you wrote. She left a message for you."

"What does it say, Zack?" Ethan said.

Zack looked to Horatio, who was staring at him with fraught anticipation.

"It says, *Ray, I'm sorry I lost you*," Zack said, and Horatio's face went slack. He put a hand to his face and covered his eyes, and Zack's father put his hand on Zack's shoulder and held him close.

The sound of laughter and conversation drifted in from beyond the Tower's doors; the Einsteins and Horatio stood in silence within, no one wanting to break the solemnity of the moment. Zack looked up to the medallion high above, and he thought of the message hidden within its jumble of letters, and he thought about the first time he'd seen Ann here and of how, for a moment, he'd thought she was his lost sister. And then he thought back to that night a year before, when Susan had dashed off from him and everything had turned dark. She was gone. Zack knew she was gone, and he knew that no matter how much he wished that wasn't true, there was nothing he could do to change that fact.

"You've given me quite a gift," Horatio said, taking his hand from his face and looking at Zack. "Ann. My wife. All of it. I can't thank you enough."

"Mr. Cuvallo," Zack said, "I'm glad you saw Ann. She talked about you all the time, about how she knew you would find her if she came here. And she did—and you really did find her. And I'm glad I was able to let you know about the message in the cave." Zack looked to his parents. "I miss Susan. But when I said that charm, it felt like she was here in some way."

Ethan moved to his brother and put his arms around him. "You're amazing, Z," he said. "Really. In all ways."

But Zack barely heard his brother's words because he began to break into tears—not sad ones this time, at least not completely, but ones that seemed to wash away a year's worth of hurt. It felt good to cry this time. And as he felt the arms of his brother and his sisters and then his parents around him, Zack found himself picturing Susan as she'd been the last time he'd seen her—smiling at him as she ate her cotton candy, happy to be with him, happy to enjoy something simple and sweet.

"Make sure the good survives," Zack whispered as the others held him.

"Make sure the good survives," his mother echoed. And everyone held tighter.

Twenty-Six

THE VIEW FROM THE TOWER

By four o'clock, the crowd had thinned to just a few clusters of people admiring the view of the river, the Tower was empty, and the Einstein kids were folding up the chairs and making sure all the trash had made its way into the trash bags. Horatio had returned home after spending some time alone in the Tower and then taking a tour of the mansion; he'd wanted to visit the cave, too, but had begun to feel too exhausted and overwhelmed to hike downhill to the spot. Zack promised to go with him to the cave the next time he visited.

Zack was helping Ethan take down the tables that had been set up for the food, and when they were done, Ethan went to help Miriam with some of the empty platters that needed to end up back in Juanita and Rydell's car.

"You good, Zack?" Ethan said.

"I'm fine," Zack said. He glanced across the river for a moment. "I just want to check something out real quick."

Ethan flashed him a dubious look. "Don't go far," he said. "And don't be gone long."

"Don't worry," Zack said.

With a glance at the Tower, Zack turned and began walking down the slope. It took him a few minutes to reach the flat and cedar-dotted spot where the old stump sat; and when he found it, he angled straight for the cave itself and moved the brush away from the entry. For the first time, he was entirely devoid of any expectation that Ann might be inside waiting for him; that the cave was empty was no surprise. Though as he stood in the opening and looked within, he was startled to see an envelope on the ground. He'd been in the cave two days before, and no note of any sort had been waiting. Now, as he peered at the letter on the dirt floor of the cave, he saw his own name written in pencil on its front. He picked up the note and was about to open it, when an idea came to him and he tucked the envelope into his pocket and backed out of the cave. A few moments later he was running up to the Tower; and then, his siblings still on the far side by the parking area, Zack entered the building and found himself alone.

He ascended the stairway to the second level and moved quickly around the rim of the balcony until he was at the spot where he

and Ann had first tried to figure out what was written on the medallion. The light was much improved now, since all the broken and boarded-up windows were fixed; but the spot seemed somehow just as hushed and distant as it had felt on that first occasion, just as remote. Zack looked at the medallion, gleaming in the afternoon light. He looked through the window just beside him, the same one through which he'd once seen Ann stealing back into the forest; a thicket of green met his eyes beyond the field in front of the Tower.

Zack took Ann's letter from his pocket and tore open the seal to pull out a single sheet of paper. On it, in pencil, was a message:

Zack, thank you for being my friend. When you told me you saw the flashing lights, I knew I would see my father again. I don't think anyone can really be lost forever if other people love them— and I think you really love your little sister. "Make sure the good survives." Your friend, Ann

Zack took a deep breath and looked at the medallion once more. He thought of Susan; and as he glanced out the window beside him, he saw a girl in the distance, her red hair in a ponytail, and wearing a white shirt and blue jeans. He pressed his face to the glass, hoping she would turn around and see him looking at her. But she continued walking without looking back, moving directly toward the line of trees. Zack wanted to shout or bang on the window—and then he didn't. He merely stared after the girl as she entered the woods, the green trees obscuring her form as Zack watched her depart, as Zack allowed her to depart.

I'll never forget you, he thought. And then he turned to take in the dome of the Tower and the vast open space before him that was filled with a gentle light. He heard Miriam shout something outside, and then Ruth and Ethan began to laugh.

And I'm glad to be here with my family, Zack thought. *All seven of us. The Vista Point Einsteins.*

ACKNOWLEDGMENTS

Utmost gratitude to dear collaborator and editor Christy Ottaviano—and to faultless guide, agent Rena Rossner. These two women have changed my life. Thank you to all my friends at Henry Holt Books for Young Readers and Macmillan Children's Publishing Group for their support over the past many years; and thank you to all the new friends I am making at Little, Brown Books for Young Readers, including Leyla Erkan, Jen Graham, Sasha Illingworth, and Patrick Hulse. Very grateful for the fine illustrations by Vivienne To (cover) and Petur Antonsson (interior). Appreciation to Tina Ullom, John Ullom, and Dan Ullom, whose Brick & Mortar Books in Redmond, Washington, is a haven and a delight. Above all, and as always, most everything is owed to Jacob, Olivia, and Natalie—and, especially, Rosalind.

Ben Guterson

BEN GUTERSON

is the author of the acclaimed novel *Winterhouse*, an Edgar Award and Agatha Award finalist as well as an Indie Next List Pick, and its sequels, *The Secrets of Winterhouse* and *The Winterhouse Mysteries*. The Winterhouse trilogy is available in ten languages worldwide. Ben and his family live in the foothills of the Cascades east of Seattle. He invites you to visit him online at benguterson.com.